Glenfield
Secrets

Christina Hazel Stephen

Glenfield Secrets
Copyright © 2021 Christina Hazel Stephen
First published by Black Jack Books May 2021

Cover design by Valerie Latimour and Michael Goodreid
Image by from Pixabay

ISBN 978-0-6486983-7-1

In loving memory of the family
who live on in my heart:
Mam and Dad (Mary and Arthur),
brothers Arthur and Tom
and Brian

In every country …
In every city …
In every town …
In every street …
In every house …
There is a story, a human story …
that millions of people would relate to …

This is a story about seven residents who live in seven houses in Glenfield Court.

Though it is a made-up story, we can be sure, because of the billions of people in the world, that part of the story may well be true about someone, somewhere …

in a house …
in a street …
in a town …
in a country …
in the world!!

On the outskirts of a large town not too far from the sea, a hiker ascended the hills, climbing towards breathtaking beauty. The view as he climbed made him feel it was good to be alive. Looking towards the sea, he caught sight of an eagle, wheeling above the waves. The majesty of the bird made the effort of the climb, the blisters and the sore shins worthwhile. At the top, he joined other hikers, many locals looking down on their town, trying to find their own street, or the school they had attended. He took in the spectacular scenery, then turned his binoculars towards the town. Through the binoculars, he could clearly see Glenfield Court, with the lovely blooms in every garden.

Everyone knew the street because every year it won a prize for the loveliest garden in the suburb. It was unique because all the gardens were tended by one man only. One of the owners loved gardening so much that he asked every owner if they minded him doing their garden. He couldn't believe his ears when every one of the residents gave him permission to do so. Tom spent all his spare time planting and caring for bulbs, flowering bushes and plants, so the whole street was always awash with colour. The street was quite famous among the locals, all thanks to Tom.

Glenfield Court nestled in the edge of a suburb built fifteen years previously. Although more houses were being built, the court would never lose its view up to the hills, due to being on the edge of the moor leading up to the hills. This was part of its charm for the residents, as they wanted to live in the town but be part of the countryside too. The cul-de-sac was about a twenty-minute walk to the main shopping area. It was quiet and clean, and contained seven bungalows, seven stories to be explored.

When rubbish day came around, the bin men didn't mind going into Glenfield Court, as it was the cleanest street in their round.

Wally, the head man, told all the new bin men, 'It is a pleasure to empty the bins here as all the rubbish is wrapped up; you won't find any litter lying anywhere in the street, plus on top of that, someone must wash the bins every week, even though they are never dirty. Yes, it is an honour to be the bin man for this street.'

All the bin men would laugh behind Wally's back, but they hadn't been in the job as long as he had. He took pride in his work. As Wally had always said, 'Someone has to do this job, so I may as well do it to the best of my ability. Having clean bins to empty helps get the job done.'

Every Christmas all the residents in Glenfield Court gave Wally and his crew small gifts in appreciation for their good work.

Wally once said, 'It is me that should be giving them presents,' but he never told the Glenfield Court residents that for they might have taken him at his word!

Number 1 Glenfield Court

Inside number one Glenfield Court, Helen Thomson was reminiscing. She was nineteen, it was the usual Saturday night and Helen had a date with a gorgeous boy from the city. If she had been true to herself, she would have seen that he wasn't for her, he wasn't her type – or rather Helen wasn't his type. Looking back Helen wondered why he had asked her for a date in the first place. Anyway, she was to meet him at one of the local pubs where she and some of her friends used to drink before going on to the dance at the town hall.

They all had a couple of drinks and were getting excited about the dance. Everyone looked forward to the Saturday dances for you never knew who you might meet, and gathering in the pub sharing the ritual anticipation of 'maybe tonight's the night' before going on to the dance was all part of the excitement of being young.

Of course, Helen's date was late.

Helen was looking at the clock again. She pulled her eyes away, tried to put on a happy face and join in larking with the girls. She was distracted, diverting her eyes every time the pub door opened, but it was never him.

Time was getting on. He had said eight o'clock but there was no sign of him. Helen could see the other girls were getting restless for they wanted to go to the dance but didn't want to leave Helen sitting alone. They were all good friends and had grown up together, but Saturday night was the holy night of the week especially when you were single.

Somebody had to say something soon – otherwise their evening would be spoilt. They were raring to go, no time to waste!

Eileen said, 'Are you sure you were to meet him here, Helen? It has gone past nine – don't you think he is just a little bit late? We want to go to the dance, are you going to stay here or are you coming with us?'

The rest of Helen's friends agreed. 'Yes, Helen, you have given him long enough. He isn't worth wasting any more time over. Come on, you are coming to the dance now, with us.'

A couple of the girls dragged Helen off the chair and out of the pub, laughing and singing as they went, determined that they were all going to have a good time.

By the time they got to the town hall, Helen had almost forgotten what the creep looked like. The girls thought him a creep too, although Alison called him an even worse description!

Their spirits lifted when they entered the town hall, which had been decorated with streamers and balloons. The dance was in full swing with a large crowd strutting their stuff and an atmosphere of excitement. It was sure to be a fantastic night; the girls could hardly wait.

The music was loud and inviting, setting toes tapping. The band was very popular, turning out good records regularly. They'd even had a song in the top ten. Although they hadn't yet made it to number one, the way they were playing tonight it wouldn't be long.

The atmosphere was electrifying. The girls got onto the dance floor and showed everyone what they could do – and could they dance, man! Even Helen allowed herself to be hypnotised by the magical sounds coming from the stage.

The mystical group attracted the attention of all the keen young men at the dance. Before long, all the girls were partnered off and dancing the night away, oblivious to the single girls dancing alone glaring daggers at them.

Helen didn't see the daggers and if she did, she wouldn't have cared. The night was turning into one better than she could ever have imagined.

The man who asked Helen to dance was Arthur. She knew him but she had never really spoken to him. All that changed forever, on that lovely summer evening at the Saturday night town hall dance.

Helen woke from her daydream. She felt sore sitting in her chair all scrunched up. She hadn't felt it in the cocoon of her memories, dwelling in the past. When she was there, with Arthur, she could forget her greying hair and huge size. Back in the present, she was once more depressed and tearful. She reached automatically for the chocolate.

Seven years she had lived in the house. Arthur had died four years ago, and she had never got over his death. Arthur had been her world. Helen had loved staying at home and taking care of Arthur, baking his favourite meals, knitting his jumpers, warming his slippers when he got home on cold, wet evenings from work; yes, she loved being a housewife. Helen loved being in love with

Arthur. All that changed one wet night when a drunk driver ploughed into Arthur's car as he was driving home to her. Helen's world died with Arthur. Since then Helen had never really lived. Everything was just a blur – nothing mattered anymore, nothing counted, she was alone, so what was the use of doing anything.

Once a week, Arthur and Helen would go to the beach, walk along the seashore hand in hand and pick up shells or coloured stones, whichever took their fancy. They sat at their special part of the beach, spoke about the shells or stones and watched the big waves come hurling into shore with the seagulls diving away from the swirl. They sat cuddled together and no one in the whole world could touch them. They were in their heaven. They loved the spray of the salt water playing with their faces and the breeze from the North Sea drying it before the next onslaught would happen and they laughed with one another, as they were in love and happy as one.

'If only I could get back to our beach,' she said, 'then I could be close to Arthur for a while; our beach, our special place.'

Unable to drive, all she could do was dream about being with Arthur at the beach. Arthur had said, 'You don't need to drive as I do all the driving and we only have one car, Helen. I will take you wherever you want to go to.'

'How I wish I had stood my ground and demanded that I needed to learn to drive in case of future events, like the one that I am now in.' He had been a good husband but Helen was starting to realise he hadn't given her the independence that she deserved and needed.

As Arthur travelled overseas a lot and Helen went with him, she had never had a job after they got married. After Arthur died she thought about getting a job, but she had no qualifications. She applied for several positions but no one wanted someone without experience. As Arthur left her comfortably well off she preferred to stay at home and work in her back garden or read a book, watch television and eat chocolate, which was her favourite food! When the loneliness overwhelmed her, which was often, she would walk round her home crying and talking to herself. 'What can I do to feel better? I so wish I could have someone to speak to or go out for a coffee with. I can't stand this anymore, Arthur. I miss you so much, I wish you were here, I need you.'

She must do something to make herself feel better, but what? 'What? Can I possibly do?' she asked herself, getting off the chair and going to look out the window at the flowers that were starting to bloom. 'Tom does a good job of my garden; I don't know what I would do without him.'

This particular morning as she was reading the newspaper that had been delivered to her, the front doorbell rang.

'Oh! I wonder who that can be,' Helen said, speaking to herself, as people who live on their own often do. 'No one ever comes to my door, I wonder if it is one of the neighbours.' As Helen waddled from the kitchen into the hall and along the passage, the doorbell pealed again.

'Okay, okay, I am coming,' she shouted at whoever was being impatient.

When she opened the front door, her heart fell straight to the ground. She couldn't believe what she was seeing. There must be a mistake; her eyesight was letting her down. She would have to get her eyes tested because what she saw could not be right! Helen closed her eyes and opened them again to make sure that what she saw was real. Three huge coloured balloons were tied to the gate - and what was written on them in big black texta made Helen cry.

On each balloon was printed the word FATSO for all the world to see. She heard, rather than saw the three hooligans laugh and run away round the corner.

Helen stood like a statue, unable to move. Tears were running down her face as the three balloons were swaying in the wind, the word FATSO jumping out at her. That is what people must be saying behind my back, she thought. Especially when youths take it upon themselves to remind me. She stood there for ages before Tom Murray from number four walked past. He saw the balloons swaying in the wind but didn't see the word FATSO on them as they were facing Helen.

'Hello, Helen, are you okay? What has been happening here? Is there anything I can do?'

Tom opened the gate and saw the words on each balloon. He immediately burst them with a rock that he picked up from the garden. He squashed the burst balloons into his pocket and walked up to Helen. Taking her arm he said, 'C'mon, Helen, let's get you inside and I'll make you a nice cup of tea.'

'Oh, Mr Murray, why do people have to be so cruel? I haven't done anything to them!'

Tom led Helen into the house, down the passage and through to the kitchen, sitting her down on a chair by the table, where she just put her head on her arms and kept sobbing.

'Now, now, Helen, please call me Tom. You know how kids are, they'll do anything to hurt others if they are going to get a laugh. I saw the boys run off and I know their parents, I'll go and have a word to them.'

Helen clutched Tom's arm, 'No please, Mr Mu... Tom, please don't, as they might come back again and I don't think I could stand more upsets.'

'Okay, Helen, I won't but I really think you need to have a cup of tea, now where are the cups?'

Tom put the kettle on, found the teapot, cups, sugar and milk; he was handy around the kitchen as he did a lot of the cooking at his house.

Once the kettle was boiled and the teapot filled, with milk and sugar in both cups, Helen had calmed down a good bit and said to Tom that she didn't take milk or sugar and they both laughed because Tom had forgotten and had done it without thinking as he and his wife both took milk and sugar.

'I keep the sugar in case I get visitors – but as I don't, that sugar may be years old!' Helen said and again they laughed.

Tom stayed with Helen for quite a while, talking about anything that would take her mind off the horrid experience that she had just gone through, even telling her about his life, which was taboo to anyone else. Once she had calmed down, he gave her his phone number and told her to ring anytime if she felt anxious or just wanted someone to talk to as that was what neighbours were for. Even though he only lived a few houses up the cul-de-sac, it made Helen feel safer knowing that she could phone him anytime.

'Thank you Tom, you have saved my life because when I was standing at the door looking at those awful "fat" balloons, I felt that I had had enough and life wasn't worth living.'

'Now Helen, we won't have talk like that, okay? Life is good, you just need to look around you and see for a start that you have really good neighbours, it is just a case of getting to know them. We all have our problems and we don't like to share them but maybe we should. Sometimes other people can help us better than we can help ourselves, what do you think Helen?'

'Oh yes, Tom, you are right, of course and it has taken you to speak to me that I can see what you mean. Today is going to be the start of a new life for me and even though I can only go slow, I am going to show them! Just you wait and see. Thank you so much, Tom, thank you.'

'Okay, Helen, I can see that you mean it, so I shall say cheerio for now but I am only a stone's throw away, bye, bye,'

'Cheerio, Tom,' and as she closed the door behind him she felt that a weight had been lifted from her. She knew exactly what she was to do.

'Oh, thank you again, Tom,' she said as she waddled along the passage to the kitchen and her new beginning. She even started humming to herself, something that she hadn't done for years. Helen was really on the way to a new life.

One year on. The present.

Helen was driving her new car to meet Ian at a restaurant for lunch. There were lots of puddles on the road from the rain the night before, but it had cleared up with a still-strong sun trying to peek through the clouds in the autumn day. Nature was giving them a little more of summer's warmth before the long, cold winter ahead. It had been a long hard year for Helen, but at last she had made it. She was the victor.

Admittedly she'd had help, there was no way she could have done it without help, but SHE, HELEN, had decided, had been determined, had been the one to say, 'It has to be done now before it is too late.'

Thinking of Ian gave Helen a warm glow; he had grown on her over the last year. He had helped her so much that she felt a special bond had grown between them.

'What a year! I feel so lightheaded, almost as if I had been drinking. I am so happy, I could sing, but I'd better not, must concentrate on the wet slippery roads.'

What happened a year ago

A year ago, when Tom had burst the balloons that the horrid boys had tied to Helen's gate and she had felt that there was no point in going on, she could never have imagined that so much could have happened to her.

Before that day, she felt sorry for herself, could see no future, no happiness, just cold hard days stretching ahead, waddling round and round her house, crying and wailing for Arthur, until she stopped with exhaustion and lay down still crying.

But all that had changed. It took time but once her eyes had opened and she could see that there was life outside, there was no holding Helen back.

During the year good things had happened, positive, happy, exciting things, with lots of hard work on her part, yes, lots of hard work.

The first thing that Helen did with Tom's help was to go to the doctor and get a health check-up and to tell the doctor what she had in mind. The doctor was pleased that at last she was coming out of her slump and encouraged her by giving her information about healthy eating. She was sent to the nutritionist in the rooms next to the doctors, where they would help her. The nutritionist was very helpful and she had an appointment once a week with her to make sure that Helen was eating the proper food and portions. She came away from there with lots of brochures and easy recipes, as Helen no longer enjoyed cooking.

Helen was on her way, the first step had been taken, now the second was about to begin.

Again, with Tom's help, Helen joined a gym. They took a taxi to a local gym – too far for Helen to walk to at present, but hopefully not for long. Tom's company helped Helen feel at ease as they filled in forms to get her joined up.

Helen got the taxi to the gym three times a week. She persevered with it, determined not to give up. All the trainers and people who went to the gym were extremely nice and helpful towards her and nothing was too much bother as they could see that she deserved their support.

The first few weeks Helen thought she was going to die, she felt that the instructors were holding a whip to her; she couldn't believe that people went through such pain just to lose a few pounds. Well maybe a lot of pounds in her case. After each session, one of the instructors would tell Helen how they thought she had progressed that day and even though she felt bedraggled and just about ready to drop, she perked up when the trainer was pleased with the day's effort.

Greg, a trainer that she had regularly, said, 'Helen, you don't believe how well you are progressing, do you? I see the disbelief in your face each time I tell you, but it's true, honest, you are doing fantastic for the length of time you have been here. The only thing I would like to say is take your time. You have got the rest of your life, and the way you have taken to the training, you will have a long one ahead, but just … take … your … time. Remember, you are not alone any more and we are all here to help you realise your dream, okay?' and with that Greg went looking for his next pupil.

Helen religiously went to the gym three times a week in the taxi for three months. The following three months she didn't need the taxi, but she liked Arnold, the taxi driver, so much that she kept him on. Some days it would rain so it was just as well to have a standing order. That way, everyone was happy and dry!

Helen continued going to the gym but cut it down to once a week, as her life was so full that she had barely time to read the newspaper now. Once Helen had lost the weight that the nutritionist, the doctor and the trainers felt was ideal she decide that it was time for plan three!

Helen was speaking to Tom outside her gate one day just as she had got home from the gym and so she told him about the next chapter in her life. 'I want to learn to drive. "Everyone off the roads, Helen's a comin' down the High Street," ha, ha, ha. What do you think Tom?'

Tom couldn't believe how Helen had been transformed from a mouse into a lion. 'Helen, that is the best news since you decided to join the gym. I am enjoying seeing the new you, go get them.'

Helen looked solemnly at Tom. 'Tom, I owe you everything, you know. If it wasn't for you I would still be hiding in my cocoon, waiting, for what? You saved me Tom, I shall always be grateful. Mary is a lucky woman, having a wonderful man who is so considerate, you think of other people's sadness and hurt and not many people do that Tom, you are one in a million, a true gem, thank you so much.' She kissed his cheek.

'Oh, Helen, I am not; but I have enjoyed seeing the progress you have made and Mary has too, now go get driving. I know a man at the church who belongs to a driving school, if you would like me to speak to him about you?'

'I certainly would, Tom, I would like that very much, so whenever you find out when I can have my first lesson, I shall be waiting.'

It was only a few days later that a knock came at the door and when Helen answered it she saw a man in his early fifties standing there holding a file. Before Helen could object, as she thought it was a salesman, the man said, 'Hello, Mrs Thomson, my name is Ian Munday and I am a driving instructor with Welsh driving instructors, Tom said that you might be needing our services?'

Helen was taken aback, first the good-looking man standing in front of her and then the sudden realisation, that yes, she was wanting to drive and it had to start somewhere.

'Oh, sorry, Mr Munday, I thought … well, I thought you were a salesman, I'm sorry.'

'That's okay, Mrs Thomson, I thought that's what it might have been, but I am selling something really, I am selling my time.' He laughed.

Helen was made to feel at ease, 'Ha, ha, you're right, look would you like to come in and we can discuss whatever needs to be discussed.' She laughed again. What on earth was she saying? *I am speaking gibberish, I hope he doesn't think I'm stupid, oh be quiet, woman.* All of this of course was going round and round in Helen's head as she was quite taken with the pleasantry of the man.

The next day that Helen saw Tom, she said, 'Tom, I think I made a complete fool of myself in front of Mr Munday, or he did ask me to call him Ian, he probably won't want to teach me to drive as he might think I'll end up driving on the pavement.'

'Helen, you did fine. I spoke to Ian this morning and he said that he was looking forward to your first lesson, so don't worry, he is a very good instructor, you mark my words.'

'Thanks Tom, if my hair was blonde, I would be a dumb blonde, ha, ha.'

'Margaret, up the court, has blonde hair and she is certainly not dumb, she has her own business, so there is a lot to say about blondes.'

'I know it is just such a cliché and because I have so much more confidence now, thanks to you, I often open my mouth before I think.'

As Tom walked away, he turned round to her and said, 'You will do fine, girl, you will do fine.'

Helen wanted to learn as soon as possible, so she booked two lessons a week, every Tuesday and Friday morning. She was eager but she didn't want to be rushed.

'Oh don't worry, Mrs Thomson, we won't be rushing you and you will only progress when we think you can pass your test, we aim to make sure that you will be a confidant, capable driver. You did say that you wanted to drive up to the Highlands, well you will need to do a lot of manoeuvring and by the time you have passed your test you will be able to do it blindfolded, ha, ha.'

'Yes I do want to drive there. My late husband and I went up there for our honeymoon and that is one of my goals, to see the place again and to know that I did it all by myself, but I don't want to do it blindfolded, ha, ha.'

The lessons were difficult to begin with of course, then slightly easier as the weeks flowed on until Helen was completely at ease driving with Ian beside her. Her confidence was growing too, maybe because Ian was so patient and considerate and he always seemed to know how she was feeling. Helen was a completely different person since the balloon episode, but she still felt scared at times when she saw a group of teenagers when she was driving. Ian knew about the balloons as Tom had told him so he knew exactly how to squash the feeling that were doomed to come to the surface, he just changed the subject and changed the direction they were driving. In time, Helen got over her fear until she wondered why it had been such a big black cloud in her vision.

'No more being frightened of those bullies,' she shouted out of her bedroom window one day, when Helen felt that she was nearly back to the person whom Arthur fell in love with. 'I feel nearly whole again and I look forward to what the future has in store for me, because I know there will be a future.'

Whenever Helen went up town, she would now walk. She enjoyed speaking to everyone she passed, and looking up at the trees and the birds – to just look.

She often saw Ian up town, but not to speak to as he was either in a car, or on the other side of the road, and she couldn't catch his attention. Quite often she saw him with a young woman and sometimes it would be with another man, but never an older woman. One particular day she bumped into him with the young woman while she was walking along the high street.

'Why, Helen, how nice to see you,' he said with a big smile towards her. 'May I introduce my daughter Angela? Angela, this is Mrs Thomson, one of my pupils.'

'Oh please Ian, enough of the Mrs Thomson, Angela, hello, pleased to meet you and please call me Helen.'

'Hello, Helen, yes, my dad is always respectful when it comes to his pupils. And how are you going with your driving?'

'I have my test next week and I shall be keeping my fingers crossed, ha, ha. Eh Ian?'

'You won't need to cross your fingers, you will pass with flying colours.' He smiled encouragingly.

They stood speaking for a few minutes before they went on their separate ways. Wow, thought Helen, I really like him, in fact more than like him, he knows too, and the daughter knows, I wonder if he has a wife. I shall have to find out.

It turned out later that day that Helen found out quite by accident that Ian was divorced and still single, she overheard two women speaking about him when she was in the library. She didn't hear the rest of the conversation as she was passing them at the counter. *Drat, I wonder what else they were saying; well at least I may be in with a chance. I am going to ask him out, yes I am.* Helen was determined that if she passed her test (but of course she was going to pass her test, silly!!) she would ask him out to say thank you. She saw Ian twice a week when he gave her lessons but he had never asked her out, even though Helen knew he liked her. Of course she passed her test, first time and it wasn't such an ordeal as she had thought.

'Congratulations, Helen, well done, I knew you would do it.' Ian congratulated her with an embrace and a kiss.

She was blown away, she tried to keep her composure, but that kiss, even though it was on her cheek! She smelt his aftershave and wanted to bite him. Keep cool, girl, keep cool, time is on your side, she kept thinking but said instead, 'Thank you, Ian, thank you so much for your patience and perseverance, now may I take you out for lunch to say thank you? Because I could never have done it without the kindness you have shown me.'

'There is really no need, it is part of my job, one which I enjoy doing even just to see the look of sheer delight on people's faces, such as yourself when they pass their test.'

'Ian, you know what I have gone through this last year and with your help you have made me independent and free, so please, you must say yes.'

'Okay, yes, Helen, your wish is my command, ha, ha.'

They both laughed and again Helen thought, he likes me, he likes me!

The present

Well, here she was driving to meet Ian in her brand new car. Ian had helped her pick exactly the right one, knowing what she needed and what would be suitable. He knew, he liked her, he did!!

She parked her car with sheer precision right in the centre of the lane and felt quite proud of herself. She saw Ian looking out of the window of the restaurant at her and he laughed and clapped his hands at the job well done.

'Oh, isn't he handsome, I hope he wants to see me again, I LIKE HIM!'

Ian was the first man that Helen had met since Arthur died, but she knew without a doubt that, he was 'the one'. 'I know that we haven't gone out with each other except for the odd cup of coffee after my lesson, but he is keen, he wouldn't go for coffee with me if he wasn't.'

Once seated in the restaurant, Ian remarked on the good parking. 'Well done, Helen, you must have had a very good instructor,' he laughed.

They had their meal and chatted all the way through. Helen had a thousand butterflies in her stomach, she felt Ian was going to say something. He had an excited look on his face. I wonder what it is going to be, she thought. After their coffee arrived at the table, Ian played about with his spoon for a minute, then said, 'Helen, I have enjoyed your company during the time I have been teaching you to drive and I have come to look upon you as a friend, if I may?'

Helen could hardly answer him. She was gobsmacked, as he had never said anything like that before. 'Ian, I hope you look upon me as a friend, as I too enjoy your company and friendship.'

'Thanks, well, I have something to tell you that I have been bursting to tell you for a couple of weeks now and couldn't until I told my daughter first, as she went overseas and just got back yesterday.'

Helen was thinking, hurry up, I am just about bursting myself, but she remained cool, calm and collected.

For some unexplained reason, Ian took it upon himself to take Helen's hand, which made her all the more excited and that was something that he should not have done.

'Helen, I am getting married.' The excitement in his voice was there for all to hear and one would have had to be deaf not to hear it. If he had run out of the restaurant singing, 'I'm getting married in the morning,' he couldn't have given Helen a bigger shock. She looked at Ian, without really seeing him. The bottom had just dropped out of her world, again.

I thought he liked me, I know he liked me, I thought he wanted me.

He still kept hold of her hand, not realising that if he had slapped her in the face, she would have still sat there stunned. He couldn't see the pain on her face, as he was happy, ecstatic, so wonderfully in love that everything around him was all the colours of the rainbow whereas Helen could only see dark, black days ahead, again. Helen didn't know how she managed to compose herself, but she had been given the strength by some higher power, who thankfully could see that she needed help, otherwise she would fold, fall in a heap, and Ian would be so devastated to think that he was responsible.

'Why, Ian, how wonderful, congratulations. I didn't know you had a lady friend as you have never said,' Helen said with an Oscar performance.

'Sorry, Helen, I like to keep my personal life separate from my work, but I have only come to realise that I want to look upon you as a dear friend, if I may, so now I can tell you. I have been living with Eddie for five years now and we have such a wonderful relationship that we wish to make it permanent to be looked upon as a couple. I didn't tell you sooner as we wanted my daughter to know first. I have really enjoyed teaching you to drive and I hope our coffee chats can continue in the future.'

Helen smiled, laughed, oohhed, aahhed and did what she had to, to just keep sane. She didn't hear half of what Ian said but kept thinking, He never led me on, he never crossed the line, he didn't flirt with me, he didn't tease me, he didn't suggest anything inappropriate in fun or otherwise, he didn't touch me, he was the perfect gentleman.

HE DIDN'T SEE ME!! I was only a woman to him and he was THE MAN FOR ME!!

'Oh dear, Ian, I must get out of here, I feel migraine coming on, please forgive me.' And with that, Helen went rushing out of the restaurant leaving a stunned Ian staring after her. The rain had started again and Helen ran through some puddles to get to her car, a safe haven, her cocoon, until she got home where she could hide away from the cruel world, forever, or until she felt she could face it again.

Helen drove out of the car park with the rain lashing down the car window at the same time tears were running down her face.

Number 2 Glenfield Court

Tom was working in the garden at number two Glenfield Court when Frank arrived home. Frank stopped to say hello to Tom, and they passed a few pleasant remarks about the garden; what Tom was doing and what he planned to do next. Then Frank hurried inside and closed the door behind him with a sigh of relief.

He didn't mind speaking to Tom as he was a quiet sort of chap, not nosey like some others that he could think of. Frank drove to work each day at the shire offices, and when he came home he kept himself to himself. He didn't want to get into any gossiping with any of his neighbours and he was glad when Tom had asked to do his gardening as Frank absolutely hated it. Almost as much as he hated the idea of his neighbours knowing what he was doing.

Frank went to his bedroom, feeling soothed by the pale lilac walls, the stars on the ceiling and the dusky pink of the carpet. He changed out of his work clothes and made sure that the heavy curtains were fully closed before donning a beautiful apron adorned with colourful butter-flies. He turned on some music and sang as he cleaned the bathroom, bedroom and lounge, making sure his lovely home was as clean as a new button. He put on a load of clothes to wash, looking forward to ironing them.

When the cleaning was done, Frank put on the TV to watch an old movie. The lead actress in her heels and long skirt reminded him of his mother. He'd loved watching his mum when she wore bright, pretty dresses that swirled in the wind, her high heels clicking as she walked in them so professionally. Yes, he loved looking at women all dressed up – but he had to hide that fact.

Once when he was at high school, his mum caught him dressed up in one of her ball gowns. Frank felt like a prin-cess in it, but his joy was short lived. He was so engrossed in the beauty of his reflection that he didn't hear her walk up the stairs to the bedroom. He had tried to explain that there was going to be a fancy dress party at the school, but his mum didn't believe him. Frank often wondered if his mum knew and that she was scared to even venture into that part of her brain. Best leave it unsaid? Unthought of?

His father never said anything about Frank never having a girlfriend, probably because his nose was never out of the paper. With his pipe, paper and beer, nothing else existed for Frank's father, it was his mum that noticed everything and she never let Frank out of her sight again especially when she heard him go upstairs.

Frank never dressed up again, ever, as long as he lived with his parents. It just wasn't going to be worth it. Even when his parents went on holiday without him, his mum put a padlock on her bedroom door. His dad asked her why she did that and she said, 'You never know who might come into the house while we are away.'

He said, 'But Frank will be the only one here.'

Her final reply to that was, 'Exactly!'

Frank's dad went down the stairs shaking his head and mumbled, 'Women!'

Things had changed once Frank left home and moved into a flat, but he never felt comfortable in case someone came to the door, heaven forbid his parents. Once he was living on his own he bought a computer and started surfing the net looking for information that would help him to understand the feelings that had haunted him for years.

It took him ages to pluck up the courage to even go onto those sites, almost as if he was waiting for his mum to come barging through the door, shouting. 'I know what you are up to! Put that vile thing off right now!' It appeared that all computers were 'vile things' to her. Once he got over that fear and he knew that he wouldn't ever be disturbed by his mother again, Frank was off and flying! He found out so much about why men dressed up as women and he began to understand himself a bit more and to not be disgusted by his feelings. He was okay, he was!

He began buying magazines about men dressing up as women and he saw that there were special clubs for such people. He began to get excited, 'to be free, free as a bird, free to swirl my skirt'. Frank laughed at saying such a weird statement but he felt happier knowing that he wasn't the only one that felt this way.

Frank rang a couple of the special clubs and the people that he spoke to were all nice and helpful towards him. With each step Frank took, he felt he was on the right path and was gaining confidence. He didn't go to the clubs straight away but rang one of the organisers a few times until he felt confident to approach them.

The big day – or night – arrived and Frank was so excited and nervous that as he was reversing out of his drive onto the pavement then the road, he didn't see the lady who lived next door to him. She was walking on the pavement and had to skip out of his way otherwise she would have been mincemeat.

Frank jumped out of his car and ran to her. 'Oh are you all right, I am really really sorry, please forgive me?'

Dorothy laughed, 'It's okay, honest, I could see that you were a million miles away so I was prepared for you reversing, I called out to you before you got into your car to say hello, and I could see that you had other things on your mind.'

'Oh, yes, I was thinking about something else, but that doesn't excuse the fact that I should have been concentrating, I am so sorry! Are you sure you are all right?'

'Honest, I am fine and you go and enjoy yourself with your lady friend – I am sure you have a hot date tonight, yes?' Dorothy laughed.

Frank became all embarrassed and could only stutter, 'Yes, I sort of do and I am really looking forward to it. Wish me luck, please.'

Dorothy laughed again. 'Yes, I certainly do, now go and enjoy and don't worry any more about this near miss,' and she walked away still laughing.

Frank felt relieved as he drove away and checked himself that he must concentrate on the road otherwise he would never reach the club. 'How exciting, me, going to a club, I can hardly believe it, oh I do hope I don't act silly or stupid and I HOPE I don't meet anyone I know!'

Frank had decided to go to the club in the next town, as he didn't want to meet anyone he knew in his hometown, not until he gained his confidence. He had thought for ages about what to wear, not knowing what everyone else would be wearing. Finally he decided to wear the safe male clothing he wore to work.

The meeting was held in an old Boy Scout's hall, which was used by many groups during the week. He was welcomed at the door by a man in a pale blue dress, complete with matching shoes. The room seemed full of cross-dressing men. Everybody at the club was nice to him and for the first time in years, he felt that he belonged. He felt completely at home.

The man in charge, who was called Robyn, explained the club rules to Frank. They were reassuring rather than worrying. Nothing that was said in the club was to go outside, and he was not to mention anyone's name that he had met whenever he attended. Frank thought that that was fair enough and there had to be sort of privacy for the 'girls'. Frank realised that it wouldn't matter if he did meet someone he knew, as they would value the secrecy of the club as much as he did.

Robyn then introduced Frank to everyone. There was a good crowd that night with fifteen members that had turned up.

All the 'girls' were welcoming, offering Frank any advice he needed. They had all been in that boat before, so they understood just how nervous Frank was feeling. Gee, was he feeling nervous, but good at the same time.

He enjoyed himself speaking to other girls and they had a quiz followed by tea and coffee and sandwiches. No alcohol allowed; that was one rule that was strictly adhered to due to no drinking and driving. After the tea, there was a short meeting about future events and Frank was getting excited that he was going to be doing so many things with people like him. Before he left the club, Robyn took Frank aside and said, 'Frank, could I have a word to you please?'

Frank wondered what was wrong, whether he had done something he shouldn't, but he answered with, 'Certainly, Robyn, what can I do for you?'

'Well, it was just that all the girls have got female names and I was wondering if you had decided on a female name for yourself. If you haven't, think about one for next week as you will feel more connected once you take that step, do you know what I mean?'

'Oh my, Robyn, of course, I hadn't really thought about it. Yes I do have one or two names that I have always liked but never put on myself, I shall have one for next week. And thank you for making me so welcome.'

'That's okay, Frank we are here to serve a need and you will always be welcome here, so see you next week?'

'Yes, please. Good night, Robyn.'

Robyn started locking up the hall as he said, 'Good-night, Frank, drive safe.'

At work the next day, everyone could see a difference in Frank; he was actually smiling and whistling! No one had ever heard Frank whistle before. One of the ladies in the office remarked, 'He must have a lady friend and it is about time too, good on him.'

Frank heard her and he giggled inwardly and thought, if they only knew.

The next time he went to the club, he left home in his man clothes and changed into ladies clothes in the cloakroom at the club. Everyone understood what he was doing as they too had done the same thing when they first 'came out'.

The town that Frank lived in was fairly big and had all the big department stores that the city had but he never bumped into any of the men he met at the club. It took a while for Frank to think maybe he did see the men in the street, but when he met them at the club, they were all wearing ladies clothes. 'Of course, that is why I haven't seen the 'girls' in the cafes, when I go shopping, because I don't look at other men,' Frank said to himself as he was dusting and thinking about the night ahead.

Soon Frank was going out three or four nights a week. Sometimes he went out early and other times later but he always came home in the wee small hours of the morning. Although most folk were sleeping then, the noise of Frank's Land Rover seemed to penetrate into their slumbering state.

How Frank got up to go to work was always on one nosey neighbour's mind. She was heard saying to another neighbour, 'He must sleep at work and here's me paying my rates to a council where their workers can skive off sleeping in their time, I tell you, one day I am going to go up to the shire office and complain.'

Another neighbour said to her, 'What are you going to complain about? If he was sleeping at work, he would have got the sack by this time, so don't speak a load of rubbish and leave the poor laddie alone.' With that the neighbour walked away, but she would be back another day to get more gossip from the nosey neighbour as it was a natural thing to be nosey about one's neighbours, wasn't it?

Sometimes Frank would hear the nosey neighbour ranting and raving and would smile, shake his head and just carry on doing whatever he was doing, whether it was making fairy cakes, shaving his legs or looking through dress books. If they only knew what Frank got up to in his house!

Frank enjoyed the evenings at the girls' club. He had made many acquaintances but no real friends. Many of the girls at the club were married and the club was the only place that they could dress as women. There were one or two girls whose wives allowed them to wear ladies dresses at home, but not out in public.

Frank wanted to go out in public, he didn't want to just dress up as one of the girls. Frank wanted TO BE A WOMAN, forever!

It was okay to cross-dress in the club.

It was another thing to cross-dress in the street.

It was a bigger thing to dress up as a woman at work and the biggest thing of all; it was a gigantic thing to go the whole way and BECOME A WOMAN.

That was what Frank wanted. Now he knew it and there was no one to stop him. Frank's parents had passed away a few years earlier and his brother was broadminded, so Frank had no fear of retaliation from any member of his family.

He had a long road to travel down to make his dream to come true.

The first thing Frank had to do was to make an appointment to go see his doctor and take it from there. Frank definitely felt better having decided what he wanted and searching so long in his brain, for what he knew to be right, true, correct!

It had always been there: he was meant to be a woman!

He had known it for as long as he could remember, he knew there was always something and now ... now ... now! HE KNEW!

Relief flooded over him and for the first night in years, Frank slept soundly, at peace with himself.

He knew that the road ahead was going to be a hard one, people were going to mock, shout, jeer, laugh; some would even spit at him, but he was prepared to go through that for the feeling of being whole at the end of the ordeal. He was prepared for all that just to become A WOMAN.

One evening at the club, once Frank was sure that he could trust Robyn, he approached him and asked if he could have a word in confidence to him.

'Certainly, Frank let's go and get a coffee and sit in that empty booth, we won't be disturbed there.'

Once seated with their coffees Frank related to Robyn everything that he had been feeling and thinking over the past few years and finally deciding that the one thing he wanted most of all was to become a woman – or as near to one as possible. 'And I've thought about a female name for myself. I'd like to be called Lisa.'

'Are you sure you want to do that, Fr– Lisa?' Robyn asked. 'Do you understand all the complications that could arise from such a huge decision? One of the girls here at the club went ahead and had the full transition and she had nothing but trouble afterwards. She had gone to a psychiatrist to make sure that it wasn't just a whim and even the psychiatrist was convinced that he knew that that was what he fully wanted. About a year after the operation, Marvin woke up one morning and realised that she didn't want to be a woman any more.

'Now Marvin goes round clubs like ours to speak to the girls who think they would like to go the whole way and become a woman. He gives talks about how he felt, what he thought and what he did because he knows that that is what the 'girls' who want to change are thinking and feeling.

'Quite a few girls turn up for his talks and the majority who wanted to change, change their minds after hearing

Marvin tell of his experience. Lisa, it is one thing to cross-dress, quite another to go through with sex reassignment surgery - that's for the rest of your life. Why don't you go along to one of Marvin's talks when she next has one? It won't do you any harm but it could if you don't hear what she has to say.'

After a few moments dwelling on Robyn's words, Frank said, 'Thank you, Robyn, that is very kind of you to be so concerned. I know I am quite sure in my decision and won't change my mind. But as you have been a good friend since I joined the club, yes, I shall go along to one of Marvin's talks - on the condition that you accompany me, please.'

One year on.

It was coming into autumn and the leaves were falling off the trees like a mini whirlwind. The nights were drawing in but it was still warm. There was only a hint of much-needed rain in the air, following a summer that had been hotter than usual. Tom dutifully tended to the gardens, agreeing with everyone that they were crying out for water. With restrictions on the watering of gardens, everyone was praying for the heavens to cry.

Only one person in Glenfield Court hadn't noticed that his garden wasn't as blooming as usual. Frank could be forgiven for not being aware as he had things on his mind.

When the doorbell rang, Frank thought, that'll be Tom. I haven't answered that card he left me. But when he answered the door, he found Robyn there.

After the talk with Robyn all those months ago, Frank had seriously thought long and hard about Robyn's words.

Frank was sure about what he wanted but maybe Robyn had a point. He had to be absolutely certain as there was no turning back, but he knew without a doubt that whatever Robyn said, it wouldn't make any difference to his decision. Frank felt that he owed Robyn the courtesy to go and listen to what Marvin had to say.

Even though his work hadn't faltered, his colleagues had noticed that he had gone back to the Frank that he used to be. One of the girls said 'His love affair must be over. Poor Frank, we shall have to be extra patient with him. I wonder what happened, but it is funny that we never saw him out with a girl, isn't it?' and they gave allowances for his absentmindedness.

Even Tom noticed a difference in Frank. Respecting Frank's privacy, Tom didn't intrude, keeping to the topics Frank was happy to speak about – the garden, weather and politics. Tom had mentioned to his wife, Mary, about a year ago 'There's a real difference in Frank. He is definitely happier, even has a spring in his step. Could it be a woman?' But no one in the street had seen Frank with a female.

Yes, thought Tom, something has happened to upset Frank. He had even gone to Frank's door and knocked but received no answer; so Tom put a card through his letterbox, saying that Tom and Mary were concerned about Frank and if there was anything they could do, to please come over to the house.

Of course, Frank wouldn't and couldn't burden them with his problem. No one could help; this was something only he could work out. Frank wondered what would have happened if he hadn't gone to speak to Marvin. 'Would I have been floating blissfully on a cloud of happiness that I had been after joining the club and meeting the girls? I was so happy planning for the future to become a woman. Now, that has all changed, listening to what Marvin had to say put doubts in my mind that I didn't have before.'

When Frank and Robyn went to one of Marvin's talks, it was mind-blowing; Frank couldn't believe all the negative, sad things that Marvin had to say. She didn't say one positive thing even though before Marvin had had the operation, she seemed to be as happy as what Frank was feeling now. Marvin was back to wearing all men's clothes, so no one could mistake him for a woman as he still had a male voice, features and a male gait too. Marvin advised anyone experiencing gender dysphoria and thinking about having the irreversible operation to go and get some counselling from a psychiatrist for at least a couple of years.

Marvin also suggested a Real Life Test — to live as a woman full time, outside their home, even cross-dress for work, in fact to throw away all their clothes and buy only ladies clothes. That was one way to help determine if what they really wanted was to become a woman, any doubts about dressing as a lady outside their home would be a huge factor that they didn't want to go the whole way.

Marvin went onto say, 'For most men, all they want to do is to dress as a woman in their homes or to go to the club where they meet like-minded people and that is enough for them. There are a few, a very few, mind you that think being a woman twenty-four hours a day would be great, just because they do it for a few hours a week. Even though I had counselling and dressed outside as a lady, for a couple of years, I never hesitated about what I wanted. The psychiatrist said I had a stable, mature mind and couldn't detect any negative thought I might have.' Marvin appeared to be tiring, but he finally said, 'Please just make sure and come and speak to me as often as you feel you want to. I don't want you to make the wrong decision like I did.' Marvin went onto speak for nearly an hour with people asking many questions. Frank and Robyn left the meeting without speaking to Marvin. Feeling unsettled, Frank just wanted to get out of there quick.

'I can't believe what he said, Robyn. How sad – he is hurting so much but is prepared to help others, to stop them doing the same. But I know that I will never be like that, I know, I am sure, but thank you all the same for taking me to listen to him.' Frank was very insistent even though it was upsetting to hear how Marvin's life had been wrecked.

Unbeknown to Frank, Marvin having the operation hadn't wrecked his life; it had made him a better person, even though it took about two years after the operation to come to terms with what he had done. He had accepted it and had learned to live with the consequences. It hadn't all been doom and gloom for Marvin, he met a lady who accepted him for what he had become and she had become his rock. He spoke to men to let them see what could happen if they took the final step, as there was no going back. He was concerned for them and he spoke to them as truthfully as he could. Frank didn't ask any questions.

So much had happened in the year since Frank spoke to Robyn about his feelings that he felt like a different person. The psychiatrist Frank had been seeing for counselling every couple of weeks was pleased with his progress. He felt Frank knew exactly what he was doing. Still Frank didn't feel quite right. He couldn't put a finger on it and even told the psychiatrist.

'It is just nerves, Frank. Once you come to the decision that you are going to have the operation, the nerves will go. You have never mentioned any negative thoughts to me, but just go home and write down everything that you feel negative about and everything positive about your decision, and I shall see you in a fortnight.' The doctor was optimistic in his sessions with Frank and wasn't concerned about his state of mind, he was okay, was Frank.

Frank still went to the club every week and dressed in ladies clothes at home instead of at the club. Even though it was still summer he took a chance that no one would see him drive out in his car with his wig on. He nearly got caught one night when Helen was hurrying up the street, but she was so engrossed in a conversation with someone that she didn't bother looking towards his car.

'Whew, that was close; certainly don't want her to see me as it would be all over the street, if not the town.' Frank, as usual, spoke to himself, which he had been doing more than ever since he had been to listen to Marvin. 'But then why should I be bothered, because once I have my operation, everyone will know,' he said, but not convincingly.

Robyn asked him every week at the club how he was doing and whether he felt any better, as everyone had noticed that Frank had changed after listening to Marvin.

'Yes, Robyn, thanks, I feel pretty good this week. Look, I even came out in my lady clothes, so that tells you something, eh?' Frank laughed nervously.

Robyn wasn't convinced, but he let the subject drop. He was there to support Frank and all the girls were behind him too. They had their usual quiz night, which made everyone jolly, with lots of laughs at the funny answers some gave.

'Robyn? It's Fr– Lisa. I hope it's ok for me to phone you.'
  'Sure Lisa, what can I do for you?'

'Can you come to my house? I need to talk to someone.'

Robyn had never been to Frank's house and wondered if he was okay as it seemed important and urgent. Privacy at the club meant no surnames, and telephone numbers were only given out by mutual agreement, so Robyn never knew where Frank lived until that phone call. As it turned out they lived at different sides of the town, but it didn't take Robyn long to arrive at Frank's house. Frank was dressed in his man's clothes and Robyn thought that he was a fairly handsome man and Frank thought the same about Robyn, as he had only seen Robyn in ladies clothes.

'Come in, come in, Robyn, thank you so much for coming over so quick, I really appreciate it, would you like a cup of tea or coffee?' Frank was speaking so quickly that Robyn could sense that he was nervous.

'Coffee please, Lisa.'

They went through to the kitchen where they made small talk until the coffee was made and then they took it through to Frank's lounge.

'Sit yourself down, please, Robyn. Biscuit?'

'Thanks, Lisa, yes I shall have one,' said Robyn as he sat on a comfy chair by the window. 'Lovely garden you've got. You must enjoy gardening.'

Frank laughed. 'I wish, no, one of the neighbours does everyone's gardens as he enjoys it. I help him a little bit, but I'm no gardener.'

'Well, Lisa, you rang and wanted to speak to me, what is the matter? Anything I can help you with?' Robyn felt he had to open up the conversation, seeing that Frank needed a help to get going.

'Yes Robyn, I do want to speak to you and I am very nervous about what I want to tell you. Not nervous exactly, just scared to hear what you might say. I will get it off my chest now before I change my mind.' Frank wrung his hands, beginning to feel hot and sweaty.

Robyn set his cup down and leaned towards Frank, looking him right in the eye. 'Lisa, just calm down and take a deep breath. There's no hurry to tell me anything, just relax and tell me in your own time.'

'Thanks, Robyn, you have been a very good friend to me and I really don't know what I would have done without your friendship, even though everyone at the club has been supportive. Okay, I feel calmer now, yes, I do. Well, Robyn, I have decided to have the operation and am going to Spain in a couple of weeks to have it done there. I have looked into everything, as Marvin gave me some organisations to get in touch with to help me with the procedures, etc.' Whew, thought Frank, I'm glad that is off my chest.

Robyn just sat and looked at Frank, digesting everything he had said. Although he had plenty more to say, the initial remarks had been spoken at last. After what seemed to Frank like minutes, which in fact was just moments, Robyn stood and said, 'Frank, I am glad that at last you have come to a decision. You will feel lighter, relaxed, not stressed or anxious; and you and only you can know how that feels. Whatever happens I just want you to know that I will give you all the support that you may need and the same goes for the girls at the club.'

'Thank you, Robyn, that means so much to me. Not having anyone here to confide in makes keeping it to myself unbearable.'

Robyn wanted to know more, but didn't want to pressure Frank too much. 'When did you feel that you had come to a decision, Lisa?'

'Well, it was about a month ago actually. I woke up in the middle of the night and it was as if someone was in the room with me, I couldn't see anything, just felt a presence. I felt that something or someone was saying that I was doing the right thing, that it was the right thing for me. Honest, Robyn, I felt as if a heavy burden had been lifted from my shoulders. I felt scared and excited but kept a lid on it until I spoke it over with my psychiatrist and started organising it, so you see, Robyn, at last, I am nearly there, at last I have nearly come through the storm, the darkness, and soon I will be ME.'

'Why Lisa, I am pleased for you, now do you have anything stronger? We can have a drink to celebrate your decision.'

Frank remembered that he had a bottle of wine in the kitchen and he went to get it and two glasses. 'Good thinking, Robyn, good thinking, yes, we must celebrate.'

They sat discussing Frank's decision, and all the preparation for his operation. Before long the street lights came on and Robyn said that it was time to get home to his wife.

'Thank you so much for coming over, Robyn. I won't be at the club until I get back from Spain as I am going over there in a few day to see the doctors first.'

Robyn shook Frank's hand just before he went out the door, 'Now remember, Lisa, you have my phone number, give me a ring any time you need to speak, any time now, okay?'

'Thanks once again, Robyn for all your help, and yes, I shall phone you.'

Frank stood at his door and watched as Robyn got in his car and drove away. He looked up at the night sky, which was full of stars, a good omen, Frank thought. The street was quiet and the houses dark, except where beams of light peeped through curtains that weren't quite closed. Frank went up to his bedroom, lay on his bed and cried, cried as he had never cried before. The relief was so powerful that it drained him and all he could do was let it all out, crying until he fell asleep.

He woke in the wee small hours of the morning feeling cold. He reached over and covered himself with the doona before falling asleep again until mid-morning.

Present time

A few weeks later Robyn, not hearing from Frank, rang his telephone number, but no one answered. Robyn considered going to the house, but he was reluctant to go uninvited. He spoke about it to the other girls and even to Marvin, as privacy was a number one rule at the club. Marvin said, 'Well, you seemed to be pretty close to him, I think that in friendship you should go over. If he answers the door well and good, if he doesn't leave well alone until he makes the first move. His neighbours will know if he is at home or not.'

'Yes, Marvin, you are right, I shall do it tonight.'

So that is why at 6.30 pm on a dark autumn evening, Robyn found himself ringing Frank's doorbell after seeing a light coming from the living room window. He waited what seemed like hours but was in fact three minutes until Frank's front door opened. Oh, Frank, Lisa, you look absolutely terrible, Robyn thought.

Robyn asked rather nervously, 'Hello, Lisa, I hope you don't mind me coming over but we were all concerned that we hadn't heard from you and hoped you were okay.'

'Hello, Robyn, yes, I am fine. Would you like to come in?' Frank said, his voice emotionless as he turned away from the door and shuffled along the hall towards the lounge.

Robyn stepped into the house, closed the door and followed Frank, thinking how odd Frank looked.

Once they were both seated in the lounge, Frank went straight into his story. 'Well, Robyn, I didn't have the operation after all, I am absolutely devastated and I shall never get over it.' And he broke down and cried unashamedly.

Robyn remained calm, unable to believe what he was hearing, and feeling rather embarrassed at Frank's outburst. 'Frank, am I hearing correctly? What on earth happened? You were so sure you wanted to have the operation.' Robyn stopped, seeing how upset Frank was.

Once Frank had calmed down, much to Robyn's relief, he continued. 'Robyn, when I got to Spain, the doctors gave me a health check all over, which they do before every major operation and my check-up was no different to any other, except when it came to checking my heart. They found a weakness in it that having any major operation would be fatal and that I wouldn't be able to get through it. To put it bluntly, I would die on the operating table, as simple as that. Give them their due, they did extensive tests, even getting a heart specialist to look at me, I even went and got a few other opinions as I wanted to be absolutely sure that there was no mistake. I still can't believe what I was told by the doctors and specialists. The answers were all the same, all tests all concluded that no operation was advisable, pure suicide, if I went ahead, but of course they would never have contemplated doing it after they found out the results. I can live a normal life the way I have been doing, but I can never ever become the woman that I know I am, I am a prisoner in my body, never ever to be released. A prisoner, screaming to become the one thing that I want more than anything in my life. To become the real me.'

Number 3 Glenfield Court

'What time will you be home tonight, Leslie?' Dorothy Young asked her husband as he was leaving for work from number three, Glenfield Court. 'There's an extra art class, that I wouldn't mind going to, someone is coming to give us a demonstration on a new technique. It is an early class, starting at 6 pm.'

'Look, Dorothy, I might even go for a run after work, as the nights are getting lighter. Just leave tea, and I'll get it when I get home, okay, dear?' Leslie gave Dorothy a kiss on the lips and a warm embrace as he walked out the door.

'Thanks, Leslie.' She returned his kiss. 'I'll go earlier to help set up. See you when I get home, I won't be late, bye.'

'Bye, love.' Leslie closed the door behind him.

It was a busy day at the bank where Leslie was a manager. A few of the staff were off ill, and before Leslie knew it, it was closing time. He changed into his running gear and drove into the hills.

Leslie was a member of a running club that met in the hills every Sunday morning, and during the week in summer. There were sixty members in the club, with varying levels of fitness and commitment. Leslie loved his running and was very fit. He had been a champion runner, and had even run in the Commonwealth Games. Although he didn't win a medal, he was very proud to have represented his country.

Three other cars pulled up as Leslie parked, with runners who'd had the same idea as Leslie. After a few words about where to go, they set off. The other three runners were Phil and Bill who had been in the club as long as Leslie, plus a new woman, Fay, who had joined recently. For most of the time, they ran in single file due to the terrain and that was the best way, as one can't have conversations when running.

When they got back to the cars after an hour's run, Phil suggested they go for a drink.

'Sure, there's no need to rush home, Dorothy's at her art class,' Leslie agreed. They only had one drink as all were driving, but Leslie enjoyed the change in his routine and different company than he encountered during the day. They left to go home, planning to meet another night before the weekend. By the time Leslie got home, he was hungry, so he heated up the lovely meal that Dorothy had made, and sat in front of the television to devour it. There Dorothy found him when she got home.

'Well, love, how did it go? Did you learn something new?'

Dorothy could hardly contain her excitement. 'Leslie, it was so interesting! I didn't think anything like that would be so easy yet look difficult – I really enjoyed it. They plan to have an extra night each week, would you mind if I went to that too? Honestly, if you don't want me to go I won't.'

Leslie looked at her with new eyes. She certainly had a look of freshness about her, surely it couldn't be just the painting. 'Of course you must go, but I must say something has made your eyes sparkle. Was it really stimulating for you?'

'Not stimulating ... More, I think I was in such a rut, doing the same water colours, that I didn't think I would enjoy doing something different. But I do. Would you like a cup of tea now?'

'Yes please, love.' Leslie continued watching the television while Dorothy went to make a cuppa.

The art class fifty-one-year-old Dorothy attended met every Wednesday night, and sometimes at the weekend. The class had twenty-three budding artists, both men and women, so sometimes twice a week was called for. They had even had a couple of nude models. Although the ladies were embarrassed to begin with, they soon got over the shock and were able to concentrate on the actual painting. They held exhibitions of members' works once a year, and Dorothy had sold a couple of paintings at these exhibitions. Leslie had bought one to hang in his office at the bank.

Dorothy went to the two night painting classes that started at 6 pm, so Leslie came home to an empty house both nights. He didn't mind Dorothy having an interest, he had just got used to her presence when he got home from work. When the extra class had been going for a few weeks, he had even cut down on his running during the week just so that they could spend a couple of evenings together. I am not jealous or being childish, he thought, but I miss her being here. I know, I'll suggest the pictures tomorrow night to let her see that I appreciate her, don't take her for granted. He felt better with his decision.

When Dorothy came home with a glowing smile, he felt an outsider. Clearly, she was enjoying other people's company, but he asked her anyway. 'Did you have a good evening love? As you certainly look it.'

Dorothy realised that Leslie felt left out and went over to kiss him. 'Yes, I really enjoy the way I am painting now. I'm sorry love, am I gone too much? I will stop if you really want me to, only go one night during the week.'

'No honestly, it is fine, I just felt a bit lonely. I will get over it. Would you like to go to the pictures tomorrow night? There is a good film on uptown.'

'Oh, Leslie, I promised I would go sit with Mary as Tom has a meeting. Cheryl, the cleaning lady who usually sits with her, can't do it, so I offered. I hope you don't mind. You can come sit with us if you'd like?'

Hell, thought Leslie, but said, 'No it's okay, we can go another night. No I won't be a gooseberry while you two woman natter on about neighbours.'

'We don't gossip about the neighbours, well … not all of them, but there is something weird going on at number five, you know the blonde woman who lives on her own, she…'

'Hold it right there Dorothy, if I want gossip, I'll read our national papers which are full of it.' He laughed.

'Ha, ha, ha, okay, I get you, now would you like a cuppa?'

'Yes,' said Leslie as he headed to the kitchen, 'but I think it is my turn.'

Leslie decided to go running after work the same nights that Dorothy had her painting class. He wondered why he hadn't thought of doing that before. It wasn't the usual night for the other runners but it didn't matter. He enjoyed running on his own, that way he could think better. So it continued for another few weeks, both suiting each other, still Leslie noticed that Dorothy had a glow about her that he daren't ask why.

Sometimes she would say, 'I have to give a lift to one of the artists, take him home again, so I might be a wee bit late, so don't worry.'

Leslie hated feeling suspicious. He tried to put it out of his mind, but other than following her there wasn't much he could do. He would just have to wait and see, not appear anxious when she came home or be too inquisitive.

Leslie enjoyed his solitary running in the evening, trying new places every week, as there were plenty of hills around the town. He often saw other runners to say hello to. Running in the hills just before the sun went down was something he would never tire of. The colours on the hill, blended purples, blues and greens were like a mystical aura, bringing him feelings of peace and calmness.

One evening as he was half way round the route he was taking, he bumped into Fay, the new lady at the club. She was watching the sun getting lower in the sky, giving a lovely hue on the surrounding hills.

'Why, hello there, what are doing way up here on your own?' he asked. He thought it was a bit solitary for a woman on her own.

'Hello Leslie, isn't this beautiful scenery? I love looking at it. Oh yes, I wanted to expand the area that we always run, to explore other sections. I have been doing it for a few weeks now, never running into any trouble. I have my pepper spray, and I've got a black belt in karate, so I feel safe enough, but I am not going to do it much longer.'

Leslie felt responsible for her as they were in the same running club. He said, 'Yes, I agree, that is why I love running up here. So, if you are not going to do it much longer please let me run with you, as I would feel better knowing you are not alone. If I hadn't bumped into you, I wouldn't worry, but now that I have, I would worry about you running on your own up here in the rough terrain. Why aren't you going to do it for much longer?'

'Well, I wouldn't want you to spoil your run worrying about me, so yes I shall allow you to accompany me. I'm going to be working evening shift at the hospital but I shall still run on Sundays.'

Leslie felt better. He smiled as he said, 'Well, let's get going as it will be getting dark soon, we don't want to waste a single ray of light, now do we?'

Fay laughed too. 'No, we don't! Race you to my car?' and away she sped.

Leslie and Fay ran together twice a week for the next few weeks. They exchanged phone numbers and had coffee together after their run. Their conversations were mostly about running – their running goals, how much they'd improved, places they wanted to run. They didn't speak about their personal life as this time running together was their time, they didn't want anything to interfere with it.

Leslie didn't mention Fay to Dorothy. There's nothing to tell, he thought. She's got her little secret so I'll have mine. Leslie still got home before Dorothy on both nights. After class, she often gave a lift to one of the artists – but she still never spoke about him. That secretive way she had about her when she came home hurt Leslie but still he refrained from questioning her. He preferred to remain in the dark.

Eventually, Fay stopped running during the week but Leslie continued running on his own. Occasionally another club member would join him, but he preferred to be on his own again. The solitude in the hills suited him; he could think better on his own and plan his future.

Alone in his office at work, Leslie thought, I wonder what she is doing now. He picked up the telephone and dialled.

'Hello.'

'Hello to you too. I was just wondering what you are doing, if you have time for a coffee. Maybe by the duck pond, you know, on Leighton Road where we went before?'

'Okay, this is a nice surprise. I'll meet you in an hour, would that be okay?'

'Definitely, see you then.' Leslie felt better now, as he had something to put to her, what better place than in the park with all the flowers in bloom.

Leslie often wondered what she was doing. He would ring her on the spur of the moment and they shared many coffees. Other commitments kept them busy in the evenings, so stolen half-hours for coffee were better than nothing.

Life went on as usual, both Leslie and Dorothy busy with work, painting running, entertaining, until one evening they got a telephone call from their daughter. Brenda had moved to Edinburgh when she got married, while their son, Bob, had emigrated to Canada. Even though their children had moved away, they were in contact every week, with visits to Edinburgh often to see the grandchildren.

'Why hello, darling, it's so nice to hear from you, everything all right?' asked Dorothy

'Hello, Mum, yes, everything is fine here, it is just that Harry is going to Germany on business and he has the chance to take me. It is only for a week, I was wondering if you would be free to come up here to look after the children. I don't want to take them out of school, and it would give Harry and me a chance to be on our own. Could you, please?'

'Brenda, I would love to do that. I am sure your dad could come up too, as we both have plenty of leave owing to us. Just a minute, I shall ask him, when is it for?'

When Dorothy told Leslie the dates that they had to go to Edinburgh, he said, 'Sorry, Dorothy, but that is the week that the big wigs are coming from down south for a conference. I would have loved to go, but not this time. Will you be able to manage two little rascals on your own?'

Dorothy was a wee bit put out, as she would have loved to have Leslie with her. 'Of course I can manage. It's just that it would have been nice, up there together.'

'We shall do it soon, I promise, now put our daughter out of her misery, tell her you shall be up on your broomstick, ha, ha, ha.'

'Oh, you wicked man,' Dorothy laughed, before telling Brenda that she would be there when needed. Dorothy was concerned that Leslie wouldn't be able to cope on his own even though he was a great cook, but actually, she was hoping that this separation would make him miss her.

'I will be fine, love, it is only for a week. I shall get plenty of reading done, also get to watch my programs on the television,' he said, although he thought, mmm, I wonder? I wonder if I should? His mind was not on anyone in that house!

The first couple of days that Dorothy was gone were busy at work for Leslie, due to the conference, entertaining the big wigs at night, making sure everything ran smoothly.

Everything was running smoothly except Leslie's running up in the hills, which he decided to fix on the third night. There were a few people running in the hills, he wanted to have some solitary time but as it was a beautiful area he couldn't expect to have it all to himself. He was busy daydreaming, he didn't see the figure coming towards him through the trees, and so he careered right into her.

Wham, she went crashing to the ground, luckily not injuring herself. Leslie yelled, 'Oh, my goodness, I am sorry, so sorry! Are you okay, are you hurt? Have you broken anything? Oh, I'm sorry. I wasn't concentrating. Here, let me help you up.'

The woman shouted angrily, 'Leave me alone until I feel if I have anything broken or sprained. I just need a minute. Did you forget to wear your glasses or something?' She was still fuming until she looked up at Leslie properly as he looked at Fay. They both started speaking at the same time with laughter a close second.

'Well, this is one way of falling for you ... oh, I didn't mean that, it was just funny the way it happened.' Fay was embarrassed as it was the first thing that came into her head.

Leslie was angry with himself that he had collided with Fay, but chuffed at her remarks. 'Look, Fay, I am not offended at all, but how are you feeling, are you injured, do you think?'

'Actually, my pride is the only thing that is hurt, I too should have been concentrating, but I too was thinking of other things.'

Leslie helped Fay up onto her feet. 'So, we were both at fault for maybe thinking about things that we shouldn't have, do you think?'

Fay's heart was beating like an orchestra of drums. She couldn't believe this was happening to her after thinking about Leslie for months. He took her in his arms, holding her so close to him that she could hardly breathe. He kissed her on the lips so tenderly, she thought she was going to float up into the sky, she was dreaming, floating, she must be. Wow, that kiss.

Suddenly, Fay broke away from Leslie, 'I'm sorry, please forgive me, I have to go, I am going to work soon, I...'

Leslie took her hand, 'It's all right Fay, I'm the one that should be sorry, but I have been wanting to do that for a long time. C'mon, let's get you back to your car, where is it?'

Leslie helped her back to her car, which wasn't far. Neither spoke until they got there and it was only Fay saying, 'Thanks, Leslie, now I must go. Please put this behind us, okay?'

It was a few moments before Leslie could reply. 'If you wish, Fay. I know that you're right, I am sorry for my foolishness. It must be the spirits in the hills making me do it.' He laughed feebly at his feeble excuse.

Fay got into her car without saying anything. Leslie watched her drive away, until the car was out of sight. A million things went running through his head but at the same time, he felt like a vacuum. How long he stood there he wasn't sure, but he wasn't in a hurry to go home. There was nothing there.

Present day

The autumn morning started out cold, with the sun trying to break through the thick clouds. By afternoon it had changed into a warm day bringing people out to go for walks in the parks or wherever took their fancy.

Dorothy was at her Saturday art class, so Leslie didn't have to make an excuse about where he was going. Leslie was meeting Fay up in the hills, their favourite meeting place. They had discovered a few secret places the other runners never ventured near, where they wouldn't be disturbed.

They met when Dorothy was at her art classes on the weekend and in the evening. That way there would be no lying to say where he was going. When Fay was on evening shift, they would snatch a few moments together during the day once or twice a week when Leslie was at work. He would tell the bank staff that he had an appointment.

Dorothy rarely rang Leslie at work but if she did, it was always on his mobile. So far they had never been caught. How they had got away without being seen for this long, Leslie couldn't work out. Of course, they had been very careful, had even gone to another town once. Even at home, he was on edge quite a lot thinking maybe Dorothy had guessed but she remained the trustworthy wife she had always been. Leslie felt sick with guilt all the time.

He had tried to break it off with Fay many times, but the electricity between them was too strong. And she never wanted it to finish.

Leslie arrived at their meeting place before Fay. He sat on the grass looking at the beautiful view before him. This had always been one of his favourite places. He used to come here alone before he met Fay. He would have loved to have shared this place with Dorothy, but she didn't care for walking in the hills. It was Fay who appreciated what he loved, that was one of the reasons he had fallen for her, he thought.

He was deep in thought when he heard, 'What are you thinking about, my sweet lover? Me, I hope?' Fay had crept up behind him and kissed his neck before he could turn around and embrace her.

'What? Where did you come from? I didn't hear your car.' He was surprised that she had managed to creep up on him like that. 'You gave me a surprise right enough.' Fay sat down beside him, kissing him on the lips as he put his arms around her, holding her close, wishing this could last forever.

'I parked further along – there was a car I recognised near the picnic area, one of the girls from work. Sorry if I startled you, but I couldn't resist kissing your neck, did you like it?'

Leslie gave Fay an odd look, before he said, 'Of course I liked it, I like every kiss you give me.' Then he jumped up and said, 'C'mon, lets go for a walk along the ridge and into the forest.' He helped Fay up from the grass before walking in front along the narrow path towards the group of trees that everyone called a forest. The forest was really just a wood but one could be hidden in the trees if one so wished. Leslie and Fay wished to be hidden in them just as they had done many times before.

They walked in silence for fifteen minutes before they came to an outcropping of rocks that looked out over the hills. Leslie helped Fay as she sat down but he kept standing for a minute, not smiling, but with a faraway look in his eyes.

'Well this is nice isn't it, Leslie?' Fay said, with a question in her eyes and fear in her voice. Something about Leslie today filled her with fear.

Still he didn't answer her need to know what was wrong. 'Leslie, are you all right? You aren't ill or anything; tell me please, you are scaring me, are you ill?' She couldn't think of anything else it could be and prayed that he would be okay, if only he would tell her what the ailment was.

'Fay, I have something to tell you...'

A *year before*

After kissing Fay up in the hills, Leslie managed to get his thoughts back to some normality. No one would have guessed that he was craving another woman. Dorothy certainly didn't notice a difference in him as he worked very hard to maintain a facade, still kissing her morning, evening, whenever it was expected, because he did, in his own way, still love her.

Leslie stopped running at the weekends when he thought Fay would be there. He had heard one night that she told the ones in charge that she wouldn't be back as her workload had increased.

One runner said, 'We'll be sorry to see her go as she was an asset to the club when it came to helping with raffles, quiz nights, all the fund raising. She was good fun too. Oh, well, no doubt when one leaves normally another joins.' When Leslie found out that Fay had left he started running on Sundays again. Dorothy had asked why he had stopped in the first place.

'They were making the running into nearly a whole day, I didn't want to be away for that length of time especially when I run at night too.' Dorothy seemed satisfied by this. She appeared to still be enthralled with her painting. That was good, as she hadn't noticed Leslie's unusual behaviour. As the weeks went by Leslie got into a pattern again running on Sunday, also once or twice weeknights depending on the weather and on Dorothy's painting roster.

One day when he had a day off from work and Dorothy was working at the library, Leslie decided to go for a run in the hills. He went somewhere different as he didn't want to risk running into Fay. He was thinking less and less about her due to the fact that he hadn't seen her since that kiss.

Leslie parked his car in the picnic car park when he saw there were a few others there. Other people with the same thought as me, no wonder, the weather is gorgeous for running, the hills so inviting, he thought. Leslie was at peace when up in the hills. *I can be myself, don't have to pretend to try to fool others, wondering if Dorothy can see through me. But I am not hurting her, we stopped in time, thank goodness. Dorothy is too good a woman to hurt.* With that thought out into the universe, Leslie started running into the comfort of the challenging hills.

Leslie had only run about one mile when he came upon a woman sitting with her back to him on the grass nursing a hurt foot. He didn't recognise Fay till he came up to the front of her. 'Fay, my goodness, what is wrong, your foot isn't broken is it?'

'Oh...'

Present day

Leslie's guilt about what he and Fay were doing ate into him. Although they had been seeing each other for nearly a year, he knew he wasn't in love with her. He knew Fay was in love with him. She told Leslie that she and her husband led separate lives and he knew she wanted him to leave Dorothy. All Leslie knew about her husband was he was retired.

Leslie and Fay had managed to get away for a weekend together a couple of times in the past year when Dorothy had gone to babysit for Brenda, to let her and Harry get away for the weekend on company business. Leslie was torn between Dorothy and Fay. Although Fay was fun to be with, there was something not complete about the affair. Fourteen months after first meeting Fay, he stood beside her on the top of the hill with the view of the town far below.

Leslie took a moment to appreciate the view he had always loved. His mum and dad, who were keen hill walkers, had brought him and his brother up here when they were younger.

Fay stood apart from Leslie, knowing that today was going to be the finish of the time spent together. She was so much in love with him that she had told her husband that she wanted a divorce as she honestly thought Leslie was going to do the same. Although he never actually said he loved her, she just knew that he did, she thought she knew! Something about Leslie today told her differently.

Taking Fay by her hands, Leslie led her to one of the seats overlooking the valley where they sat down together. 'Fay ... I ...'

'Don't! Don't say it, please Leslie,' Fay cried, fear and dread in her voice. She didn't want to hear the words she now knew he was going to say. Words that were the last thing she ever wanted to hear. 'No – no – no – please – oh please!' she wailed. 'No, oh *no.*' She clung to Leslie tightly enough to hurt him, and he had to push her away. Fay stumbled to the ground, crying and wailing and trying to grab Leslie again.

Leslie could have kicked himself for what they had done; he could never forgive himself. He managed to calm Fay down eventually and to speak some sense about what they should do to maintain their dignity. The afternoon had turned out to be beautiful, with a gorgeous clear sky. It should have been raining to match their mood. Leslie knew it was the only outcome. It couldn't go on any longer after the night before, when his wife showed him what she had painted.

Two weeks before

Leslie parked his car in the garage of his home. After leaving work early, he had bought flowers for Dorothy on his way home. Something made him do that – he used to buy flowers more often, but since Fay he was rather neglectful and got onto himself for it.

Opening the front door, he called out, 'Dorothy? Hello, I'm home.'

'Hello, darling, I'm in the sitting room. Please come through, I have someone I would like you to meet.'

Leslie wondered who it could be. He pushed the sitting room door wider to see a man about their age, sitting with a cup of tea in the best chair near the window.

'Leslie, darling, let me introduce Andy from my art class, Andy this is my husband, Leslie. Andy has been such a great help to me, steering me towards a new style of art that I recently took up and enjoy so much. I think I have found my forte.'

Leslie sat and talked to Andy, mostly about art. Leslie really didn't know much about it, but Andy prattled on not noticing the little contribution that Leslie made. It wasn't until Andy mentioned his wife 'Fay' that Leslie's ears opened up. He couldn't believe it, Fay's husband in his house and all this time his wife had known him through her art class. Heavens above! Leslie started coughing and choking.

'Are you all right, dear?' Dorothy asked Leslie, rushing towards him, concern all over her face.

'No, I'm all right, just remembered I have to ring Bob about something to do with the budget.'

Even Andy was concerned and wanted to make sure Leslie was fine before he left.

'Yes, I'm fine,' Leslie answered. 'I think, maybe, it is time for drinks, eh?'

'Yes, darling, what a good idea. Now, Leslie did you know that Andy's wife Fay does hill running just like you, do you know her?' By the time Leslie composed himself he was able to make up some half lie. 'Oh, we did have a new runner start last year, I think her name was Fay, but she didn't stay long with our section as the times suited her better elsewhere, maybe her name was Kay, can't recall, though small world then eh?' Leslie was hoping that that would suffice, whew!

'Darling, remember I told you that I gave a lift to one of the artists at night school? Well it was Andy here. He couldn't drive due to an accident and Fay was working when the classes were on. Fay is a nurse, isn't she, Andy?'

'Yes, she is and a real good one at that too.'

'Anyway, darling,' gushed Dorothy, 'There is a large art competition being held in the town hall next week, over 200 paintings entered and due to the fact that Andy said my painting could hold its own, I have entered it, what do you think of that? I can't believe it – ME – little old me, entering an art competition and in among the best too.'

Leslie went over and hugged Dorothy. She really had a few surprises up her sleeve, his wife! 'Congratulations, darling, I am so proud of you.' He gave her a big hug and kiss that he meant with all his heart.

Andy rose from his seat. 'Well, Dorothy, must go before the wife gets home. Pleasure to meet you, Leslie – I'll see you next Saturday evening at the Town Hall when the winner is announced at the art show.'

Leslie shook Andy's hand. 'Yes, Andy, pleasure to meet you too.' Funny, Leslie thought, shaking hands with the man whose wife I've made love to. He felt deflated, but kept a smile on his face.

Present day

When Fay had calmed down and realised that Leslie wasn't going to change his mind, she allowed him to explain the reason he knew this affair would never go anywhere. Leslie told Fay more than he should have, feeling that he owed her an explanation. Of course, Leslie didn't owe her anything as they both entered into the illicit affair with their eyes wide open. It was important to keep Fay calm and for them both to get things off their chests in order to cleanse the situation.

Leslie couldn't have Fay making a scene in front of Dorothy and Andy. They had to salvage something sane for all involved, to make sure Dorothy and Andy knew nothing of the affair; and he was sure they didn't. Leslie spoke at length until Fay could understand that what he was trying to explain. There was only one way to go and that was the right way. Within half an hour, they were both speaking. Fay's heart was breaking, but she had to put on a brave face if she and Leslie were ever going to speak to each other again. She loved Andy, but there was something special she found in Leslie that she knew was forever. After a lengthy talk, Leslie helped Fay into her car but didn't give her the usual kiss that he had given her for nearly a year. No more. That was finished. Get a hold of yourself, he thought. He patted the car door as Fay drove off and could see that tears were rolling down her cheeks. Leslie remembered an old saying he had heard once, 'Another time, another place.'

They (who are they?) say that there are more than one person that one can love in one's lifetime, but he knew, deep down there was only one, would always be only one, true lasting love in his life and he had nearly lost it because of his foolishness. He had got side-tracked and he would never forgive himself for that and would try for the rest of his life to make it up to Dorothy. Looking up at the lovely evening sky before heading home, he thought that it was time that Dorothy and he went up to Edinburgh together to babysit.

Driving down the hill, he wondered if the florist would still be open, as he wanted to buy Dorothy some red roses, her favourite. It was a while since he had given her roses. When Dorothy had her painting in the art competition he woke up to himself, to see what had been in front of him all this time. One doesn't always see what is in front of oneself until it is too late. Leslie was lucky – he was given a second chance and for that he would be forever grateful.

There were a lot of people at the art competition and Dorothy looked lovely in blue, her favourite colour and as it turned out her lucky colour! Leslie didn't realise how popular Dorothy was and how many people had come over to speak to her and Andy. Andy said his wife couldn't be there, as she had to work. Leslie still hadn't seen Dorothy's painting as it was in the top three which were to be unveiled by a local famous artist. Dorothy didn't win first prize, but came second. When Leslie first saw the painting, he couldn't speak, he literally could not speak.

Dorothy's painting was a portrait of HIM! Leslie! Painted for all to see by someone who was deeply in love with the subject. The love the artist felt was oozing out from every brush stroke, every corner of the canvas and from every colour – there was no doubting the depth of the artist's love. Everyone in the room could see it. There were gasps from people who couldn't understand why Dorothy didn't win first prize. The tears rolled slowly down Leslie's cheeks.

'Oh, Dorothy, Dorothy, it is the most beautiful creation.' Leslie walked over to Dorothy, held her in his arms and whispered in her ear, 'I love you very much.' The caption at the bottom of the painting read:

THE LOVE OF MY LIFE.

Number 4 Glenfield Court

Tom Murray looked at the quiet gathering and could hardly believe it was his seventieth birthday party. Time had gone so fast. He and his wife Mary had lived at number four, Glenfield Court, for nearly fifteen years, moving there after he finished serving thirty-five years in the army.

They had no children but Mary had a sister Eve who was recently widowed, and they did have plenty of friends from the church. Well, Tom did as he went to the church every Sunday, but Mary stopped going when she became ill. She lost her faith in God, but she didn't stop Tom from going to church.

Tom and Mary met at the local swimming pool when they were in their teens. Although they both went to the same school, as Tom was older, he never encountered Mary. They had both left school when they met, Tom was working in the supermarket and Mary in an office. They spent every available minute together, making great plans for the future.

Tom always wanted to join the army and Mary encouraged him, so one day as he was passing the recruitment office, Tom went in and signed up. He was really excited when he told Mary as they were having a drink in the pub. It was then that it struck Mary. Tom is going away, she thought. Oh, no, what have I done encouraging him? I'll never see him again.

'Mary, I will only be going away for a few months, then I'll be back.'

'But Tom, I'll never see you! What am I going to do when you aren't here? and you might meet some army girl, oh I wish I had never encouraged you.'

'Now, Mary, it won't be for ever and in the meantime you can start making arrangements for our wedding.'

'We-we-wedding?' Mary was gob smacked. 'Do-do you mean, you want us to get ma-married?' She couldn't believe her ears. They had spoken about their future together but had never actually discussed marriage.

Tom laughed out loud and everyone was looking to see what was going on. 'Of course, I do, I love you so much and even though I know I am going to hate being away from you, going into the army is something I know that I just have to do. We won't be separated long, as we can get a married quarter. Have faith, my wee pet.'

It felt as if Mary spent the next hour crying. She was heartbroken that Tom was going away and crying that she was happy that she was marrying Tom. *What a world, happy and sad at the same time, but that is life isn't it?*

Looking back, now, Tom couldn't believe that he had spent thirty-five years in the army. They'd had a good life in the forces travelling to many places in the world where he was stationed and they had made many friends in the process. Yes, Tom thought, on the whole they were good times.

The only sad part of their time in the army was that they desperately wanted a family. Both Mary and Tom had many tests but the doctors were unable to find a reason why Mary didn't fall pregnant. Mary kept herself busy volunteering in the local hospital wherever they were stationed, and did office work when needed. Mary always had a smile and a laugh for everyone but only Tom knew the heartache behind her eyes. They had discussed adoption, but Mary was adamant she didn't want someone else's baby, even though she would have made an excellent mother. Tom tried to argue with Mary about adopting but she was determined.

For a short time, their relationship was rocky, filled with tension over all the test results and decisions not to adopt. Tom spent more time at the base camp pub than ever before, even though he wasn't much of a drinker. The rift between Mary and Tom didn't last long, but it was enough to change his life without her ever knowing.

They were happy in their own way, they didn't bicker or fight in any way and to any outsider they would be classed as boring. 'I wonder what would have happened if...?' Tom asked himself aloud, but he hadn't, so he would never know. Part of him often thought about that time and when he did, he pushed it away to the back of his mind, only for it to resurface at a later day. He knew that he would never forget, ever.

The years went by and now they were here and he must stop daydreaming, otherwise the day would be half-gone before he did anything. Tom loved gardening. Over the years he had approached the other residents in the street to offer his services, looking after their front gardens.

The gardens were small so it wasn't as if Tom would be tending to them all day every day. It gave him a chance to be outside in the fresh air and to speak to the neighbours when they too were outside. He was amazed when all the people in the court accepted his offer. They told him to let them know how much bulbs, bushes, trees, mulch and anything else that was needed for their garden would cost and they would happily reimburse him.

Since Mary became ill she didn't like to venture outdoors much. Doing other people's gardens gave Tom the opportunity to be busy outdoors and as their house was at the top of the court, Mary could sit at the big front window and watch Tom at everyone's garden. She did like looking at the flowers and plants, and watching the trees blow in the wind. She had never been a gardener and she was quite happy watching Tom tend to other's gardens and giving him a wave now and then when he stopped to look up at her. Mary had heart trouble but she could still cook, clean, wash, iron and mend, as long as she took it easy. A lady came in twice a week to do the heavy stuff as Mary refused to allow Tom to do it.

'It is a woman's job,' she would say and Tom knew it was useless to argue. It was good company for Mary when Cheryl came to clean, change the beds and do all the stuff that Mary couldn't. They formed a friendship that made Tom glad as Mary need the fresh interaction that she got with Cheryl.

'Yes,' said Tom, 'that was one of the best things that could happen to Mary.' Of course, nobody heard him speak to himself as he enjoyed doing when he was absorbed in his gardening where he could think and speak to his heart's content. 'Funny how life works out,' he mused, 'when one door closes, another always opens, oh, well, must get on as the gardening won't do itself.'

'What did you say, Tom?' asked Cheryl on her way to clean his house. 'Are you talking to yourself again? Ha, ha.'

'Oh, hello, Cheryl, no, no, no, I was talking to my plants here, they need a little sweet talking-to every now and then, just to let them know that they are loved. That way, they will bloom longer and better than any other plant grown anywhere else in the district, am I correct?'

'I never thought of it that way, Tom. I think you may have discovered a brand new potion for your plants, maybe people should try that on each other, then the world would be a better place, yes?'

Tom laughed, 'I think you've got it, Cheryl, I think you've got it, ha, ha, ha, bye for now.'

'Cheery bye, see you at fly cup time, I shall give you a shout.'

When Cheryl had gone, Tom thought, My, she is a right bonny lassie. Then he stopped again and stared into space. *He would be about the same age, too.* After a few moments Tom chastised himself and started getting on with work in hand. *Memories!*

Tom was doing Helen's garden but hadn't seen her for a few days and wondered if she was okay, after that terrible fright she had with the hooligans and the balloons. I wish I had gone to their parents, he thought, but then again their parents would probably have thrown abuse at him, as there was no way on earth that their 'little Johnnies' would have done such a thing and then they would have told him to get lost. They would probably have a cigarette sticking out of their mouth and a can of beer in one hand, or even both hands. Tom started chuckling to himself, as he imagined how the parents would look, bleached blonde hair and the men would have huge beer bellies, smelly underarms and wouldn't be able to run twenty metres down the road. *Honestly, Tom, what has got into you today?* Tom was enjoying the nasty thoughts he was having. *Just because I am nearly seventy, it doesn't mean that I have to think like an old man, I still have young thoughts and I bet I could beat the fat, beer-bellied, chump in a race, ha, ha, ha.*

The people from the church would have been horrified if they had known what Tom was thinking as some of them were stuffy, but on the whole they were a nice bunch! Going to the church on Sundays was a blessing to Tom, he felt closer to God there and the one place where he could open up his dark secret and whisper it to the heavens. He was glad in one way that Mary didn't go anymore, otherwise she would have heard his whispering and wonder what he was speaking about and she was the last person on earth that he would hurt. She must never, ever find out and at this late stage in their lives, she never would.

Tom stopped working on Helen's garden and knocked on her door, but there was no answer. Maybe gone to the shops, he thought.

'Helen isn't in, Tom. I saw her go into a taxi about an hour ago and she gave me a wave,' shouted Chloe from number six.

'Okay, thanks, Chloe, I'll catch her when she gets home then.'

The rest of the day went by in a haze for Tom, he was thinking about so many things and yet when he stopped to think about it, he couldn't really remember what he was thinking about. Some folk would say, 'That's Irish.' At least he got a lot of gardening done and he intended to go up town the next day and would see if Mary would like to go too.

'No Tom, I don't think I'll go out tomorrow, maybe the next day. I am feeling a bit tired today, you don't mind do you? If you really want me to go we could get a taxi.' Tom and Mary played the same game every time Tom mentioned going up town and they both knew how it would end. Mary just didn't want to venture far from home unless it was to go to the doctors or hospital. Tom was okay about it as Mary had been the way she was for a few years now and they both had got used to it. There wasn't really a problem, even when it came to holidays, because they had travelled overseas so often when Tom was in the army, they both felt quite happy to stay at home. Their restless years were behind them and if Tom was honest with himself, he enjoyed going up town on his own as he felt he was on a mini holiday for the day and he looked at things as if for the first time.

He usually went up town once a fortnight as he didn't like to leave Mary too often, and he tried to go the day Cheryl came to clean so Mary would only be on her own for a couple of hours. Going 'up town' was like a breath of fresh air. He went into as many shops as he could to see new things for sale, what types of televisions were in as he was seriously thinking of buying a new one. The one they had was getting on and Tom thought Mary deserved a treat. He just knew she would like that so that would be first on his list, to look for a new television.

The day began with the sun shining in the kitchen window and that seemed a good omen. Who wants to go up town when it is cold, rainy or blustery? Tom would go in any weather, but when the sun was shining, it was better. Tom left when Cheryl arrived and then strode purposely down the court, whistling to himself and looking forward to what he might be able to buy for Mary. Some chocolates and maybe a new magazine, Tom thought, with a smile on his face.

The town was busy for a weekday, but Tom managed to get into his favourite café for a coffee and cake. It was one of the highlights of the day to sit and watch the world go by. Tom was a people-watcher and always tried to get a seat by the window so that he didn't have to squint around people to see out. Today, he was in luck, his favourite seat was vacant and his favourite coffee nearly on hand.

As Tom was people watching and drinking his coffee, a voice suddenly penetrated his daydreaming state. 'Tom, is it you, Tom? My, I haven't seen you in years and you haven't changed. I can't believe I have bumped into you today of all days.' Tom turned around at the mention of his name He saw a woman who looked vaguely familiar, but he couldn't really place her even though he stared at her.

'I'm afraid I don't recall you for the moment, sorry.'

'Tom, I am Sheila, Kath Mason's sister, do you remember me now?'

Flustered, Tom got up off his chair, and apologised to Sheila as he felt the past coming rushing to meet him. 'Oh, Sheila please forgive me, it is many years since I last saw you and my mind was far away when you called my name, how are you?'

'That's okay, Tom, when one isn't expecting someone to pop back into their life, one can get a nasty shock, eh? Ha, ha, I am fine thanks and how are you, still living in this town I see?'

'Oh yes, yes, my wife and I moved back here fifteen years ago.'

'That's nice. I came back as my brother was ill and as he was a bachelor, he didn't have anyone else to tend to him. Sadly he passed away last week and his funeral was yesterday, so I am going back down south tomorrow.'

'Sorry to hear that, I never knew him of course but all the same, a brother is your blood, isn't it?'

There was an awkward silence between the two as each wanted to broach the subject about a certain person, neither quite knowing how to do so. Eventually, Sheila said 'Kath is coming back here to live, did you know that?'

'No, I … I didn't know that, we didn't keep in contact and I thought she had gone to Canada for good. When is she coming back?'

'That's why I thought it was funny running into you, Tom. Kath is coming back here next week, she is moving into my brother's house. He left it to both of us, but we felt that Kath would be better with it as she wants to come home now, rather than us selling the house and splitting the proceeds. I don't need anything so we decided to make it a family home, that way, I can pop up whenever.'

Tom felt so flustered that he couldn't stop stammering and Sheila tried to put him at his ease. 'Oh Tom, I hope I haven't embarrassed you, I didn't mean to, look, all that was years ago, Kath was and is okay with it, so put it out of your mind. Maybe Kath was hurt but the two of you knew what you were doing so no one is to blame. Well, that is what I think. She kept the baby and everything turned out fine, he has grown up, been married and is divorced now so he, Michael, is coming back home with Kath.'

Tom felt even worse then, to think his son was coming back to live and he would be able to see him walking down the street. It was almost too much to take in. *Why did I come up to the town today, why didn't I do it tomorrow, then I wouldn't have bumped into Sheila oh, why? When everything was going well today. What must Sheila think of me, to have fobbed off my responsibilities.*

That was many years ago and he had tried to keep it squashed down. He tried to blank it from his mind, to pretend it was a dream or rather a nightmare and now, here was Sheila, saying they were coming home next week. What was he to do?

'You know Tom, I am glad we bumped into each other, because I really think you need to see Kath when she comes home. I can't explain the reason, but for all concerned I honestly think you two should talk. Your wife doesn't need to know as Kath is happy on her own, but I think you should meet your son before it is too late. Here is my brother's address, give Kath a couple of weeks to move in then go visit her. In the meantime, I shall let her know that I have seen you and what I told you and that the rest is up to you, okay?'

'Sheila, it has certainly been a bit of a shock and it will take me a few days to get over it, I really don't know what to say, I am flabbergasted. My past seems to have come flying up to me like an out of control train and smashed me right in the face. Sorry about acting like this. You have always been nice to me and you could have told my wife, but you respected Kath's wishes and for that I shall always be grateful. Thank you, Sheila.'

When Tom got home, Mary could see at once that something had come over him as his face had the look of having had a shock. 'Are you all right, Tom, you don't look well?'

Tom took hold of himself; she must never know. 'Yes, Mary, I am fine, I think I overdid it with too much gardening then walking uptown. Next time I'll take the bus.'

'You make sure you do that, Tom Murray. Maybe you should cut down on doing so much of other people's gardens, eh?'

Tom started going along the hall, 'No, I'll be fine. I am going to have a shower now, before I start tea, okay?'

Mary answered with a 'Yes, okay, then,' but thought, I know you, Tom Murray. There is something wrong and I am going to find out what it is – and maybe I do know what it is. With that, she went back to reading her book, but she wasn't really looking at it.

The present day

It was a blustery autumn afternoon with the threat of rain approaching in the big grey clouds overhead. It had been like that all day, but now, it looked as if it was going to deliver all over the people who had come to the church to pay their last respects to their friend and neighbour. The service had ended and the group were standing inside the vestibule talking quietly. There wasn't going to be a wake at the house or the pub, but instead a cuppa in the hall at the side of the church. They were waiting for Tom to move, not wanting to hurry him along or interrupt him as they could see he needed few minutes alone. He was their friend and neighbour; they owed him a lot for not only doing their gardens but also taking their rubbish bins out and in and he was there for them. Now they were there for him, hopefully.

Tom stood outside the church alone, waiting, but not sure for what. Just looking at the graves … the trees … the bushes … the sky … the clouds … Looking but not really seeing. What a funny day, he thought. Does a day have to look special when one buries their wife? I wonder. It is a funny day in a way; it is a blank day … an empty day … a day with no feeling inside. Just a vacuum, a black hole … a horrid black empty hole of a day!

What was he going to do without her? Oh, he knew he would manage to cook, clean do all the mundane things he had to do, but she wouldn't be there. His Mary, his sweetheart, his valentine, his dance partner, his lover and best friend … the one who had always had his heart and always would.

'Mary, Mary, Mary, where are you? I need you. There is a huge pain in my chest that will only be cured when once again we are together. How am I going to go on? We should have gone together. Why didn't you wait for me?' Tom thought he had spoken aloud, but it was just that his thoughts were so strong in his head that it appeared to him that everyone must have heard.

A voice penetrated Tom's thoughts. 'Are you all right, Dad?'

The voice nudged Tom back to the present. There would be plenty of time to reminisce after, he thought. Dad, the word that Tom had longed to hear, had waited thirty years to hear – and even then it was in secrecy as his beloved Mary could never know.

'Yes, Michael, son, I am fine, thank you.' Tom turned to look at Michael with pain in his eyes and a plea that said, 'Don't leave me alone.'

Michael took Tom's arm and led him into the hall for everyone to pay their respects to him. 'This way, Dad. We won't stay long, you need to get home to a warm fire, how does that sound, eh?'

Michael is a good son, thought Tom, but I haven't been a good father. He clung onto Michael for more support. 'That's sounds just grand lad, thank you. And thank you for taking care of me, I so wish Mary could have met you. I know she would have loved you. Sorry, Michael, I think I need to sit down.' Michael got Tom a seat and went to get him a cup of tea, as there was no alcohol at the church, but he could have something stronger when he got home.

While Michael was getting the tea, people gathered around Tom giving him their condolences. Although Tom was very humbled that a lot of parishioners were there, he was grateful to see his neighbours around him: Leslie and Dorothy, Alex and Chloe, Helen, bless her for coming after everything she had gone through, Frank who was practically a recluse, even Chris who had just moved, had come back for the funeral, bless her too. The only one missing was Margaret, he had really liked her before they all found out what she had done, destroying young lives with her drugs. How dared she!

Tom and Michael stayed until everyone left, then after thanking the minister, Alex and Chloe gave them a lift home. Michael stayed with Tom for a couple of hours making sure that Tom was okay to stay on his own before heading home to his mother's house.

'Are you sure you will be okay to stay on your own, Dad? I can easily spend the night if you want me to.'

Tom was adamant. 'No, no, no I'll be fine, son. You get off home to your mother and I'll see you soon.'

Michael knew Tom would be okay. 'You just ring if you feel you want me to come back. And Alex said to give him a call if you need something, okay? You have a nice warm fire and your slippers are by your chair. I'll just get you a whisky to warm your insides then I'll get going.'

'Thanks lad, thanks for everything.' When Tom was on his own, he sat looking into the fire for what seemed like an eternity, thinking about his and Mary's life together and wondered where the years had gone. A lifetime goes past so quickly that trying to hold onto a memory is like a flash of lightning in the sky.

'We had a good life together, even though we weren't blessed with children,' he said aloud before taking a drink of whisky, which was definitely the best he had tasted. 'I might have another, I am not going anywhere and it will dull the senses. That needs to happen to me tonight. Can't believe that it is nearly one year since I first met Michael and I so wanted tell Mary. I wish with all my heart that I did. Why didn't I?'

Tom thought back to when he went to see Kath, who was now living in her brother's house.

Present time

Tom was brought back to the present with the chime of the clock and thought that Mary would have definitely liked Michael. He went over to the mantelpiece where a photo of Mary was situated beside a vase of roses and picked up the silver-framed photo. 'Mary, please forgive me for deceiving you, but I was thinking of your health, I was scared that if I had told you about Michael, that you might have had a stroke or even a heart attack and I wanted to protect you. I didn't want to see you more ill than you were, you fragile flower of mine, how I miss you and love so very much.' Tom stood and looked at the photo of Mary for ages and kissed her before putting the frame back up onto the mantelpiece.

Behind the photo, leaning on the wall, was an envelope he hadn't seen before. He picked it up and saw that it was addressed to him. 'That's odd, I wonder who put that up there, instead of handing it to me. I wonder if it was Michael just to let me know that he was here for me.' It was then that he noticed that it was written in Mary's handwriting. He wiped his blurred, teary eyes with the back of his hand.

Tom couldn't understand how a letter written by Mary had been on the mantelpiece. 'I wonder who put it there, it couldn't have been Mary. Unless she put it there before she passed away and she could have. It is hidden behind her photo and she knew I would take her photo down after the funeral, Mary, Mary, Mary … My love …'

Tom took the envelope down and sat on his comfortable chair. He smelled it before opening it apprehensively. Even after he opened it he held the letter that Mary had written, in his hands, close to his heart, trying to will her back to him, to have her beside him. When he felt ready to read Mary's letter, he unfolded it gently. Knowing that Mary had touched the paper before him, he wanted to feel her presence beside him while he read it. When Tom was ready to read what Mary had so painstakingly written down (and knowing Mary, she would have read and reread every word to make sure that it was understood) he settled down to 'listen' to his love. The letter was written the day before she died.

My Dearest Tom,

I am a big coward, as I feel I have to write you a letter instead of broaching you with my intention, face to face. I wonder if I will ever give you this letter. I am writing it in the knowledge that if I am not able to tell you then I will give it to you and that our life together will be happier than it has been in the past 50 years. Don't misunderstand me, my Tom, I love you and I have loved you the last 50 years, but it doesn't alter the fact that we could have been happier. I hope this isn't going to be a shock, but I know that you have a son and have known for the past 30 years. The only regret I have is that you couldn't tell me about it all those years ago. I know you didn't want to hurt me and that is the reason you didn't say anything but I was a strong woman then, able to understand one mistake out of a lifetime that we would surely have made. Please, Tom, don't be sad, I am not.I know that he is now living here and that you see him every fortnight. I am happy for you, truly happy. I see you have a spring in your step when you come home from being up town and I cherish the look on your face. I know that you have been meeting him for nearly a year and every time you come home after being with him, I sit and pray that you will tell me about him and that you want me to meet him.

Tom, I would love to meet him, what happened was so long ago and not worth mentioning or getting angry or guilty about, please let me meet him, I know that I would love him as you do, he is part of you, so there is no way that I could possibly not like or love him. The reason I am writing this letter to you now is because I am going to try to get the courage up tomorrow to say to you, 'Tom, I want you to bring your son home here, so that I can meet and welcome him into our family.'

Wouldn't it be wonderful, Tom to have your son home here for tea once in a while? We would be a real family. I am getting so excited, knowing that it will happen. We all have regrets but one must put them away and only think of the present and the future to make plans. I am going to put this letter behind my photo on the mantel-piece because I know you won't look there.

If on the other hand, I am not able to tell you that I want to see your son, something must have happened to me, so you will most likely come across the letter when I have passed away, because I know you will pick up my *photo beside a vase of red roses on the day you bury me. Tom, please don't be sad, I love you, I will always be beside you and I want you to tell your son all about me, you and me; what you, me and your son would have done in the future as a family. Please tell your son I love him and hope he calls me his stepmum.*

My love to you for ever, Tom and thank you for my life, I could never have lived it without you.

Xxx

The letter fell from Tom's hands as his head bent forward into them.

Number 5 Glenfield Court

Margaret Shore lived in number five Glenfield Court and had done so for nearly six years. She was sixty-two years of age and lived on her own. Although she had been married years before, she was single now and had been for many years. Even though she still had a good figure, it was going in the direction of the plump side and she often thought she should do something about it, but maybe tomorrow?

Margaret had had blonde hair as a child and so she kept it that way thanks to the bottle with the occasional visit to the hairdresser. She was average height and had a cheery nature and always waved and spoke to everyone in the street when she saw them. The golden rule that she possessed was: no inviting neighbours in for coffee as that leads to being over friendly, asking too many questions and before you knew it, they would be on the doorstep day and night. No, this was not *Coronation Street* and she wasn't about to make it that way!

Margaret's younger life

Margaret didn't have an easy childhood and she never went back there in her mind. 'That was the past and that's where it will stay,' she would say to herself when she started feeling pangs about her childhood days with her mum, dad, brothers and sister.

Her dad didn't work much as he had heart trouble, which was genuine. Many men in the olden days would pretend to be 'ill' when they were as fit as a fiddle. No, Margaret's dad, Bob, was genuine and he hated being like that. He had rheumatic fever as a child and the illness made his heart weak, so much so that he couldn't work more than a couple of hours a day. Bob did work when he could get it as a watchman at night on building sites so he was able to bring home some money.

Margaret's mum, Betty, did house cleaning and school cleaning, and never seemed to be at home. Being the able-bodied one, she had to bring home regular money. Margaret had three brothers and one sister, so there wasn't a lot to eat and plenty of fighting over what scraps were left after the adults got fed.

Margaret had a fairly happy childhood until her dad passed away when she was eleven. Then things started going downhill. Her mum was tired after having to work from dawn to dusk and scrimp and save. Not long after Bob died, the butcher asked if she would move in with him and be his housekeeper. Betty wasn't sure what 'housekeeper' meant but at least there would be a roof overhead for her five children and herself, and there would be plenty to eat. It was a case of starve or survive. Betty thought hard for many nights and when the butcher asked her to make up her mind as he wasn't going to wait for ever – he wanted someone to warm his bed and to cook and clean for him – she immediately said, 'Yes.'

Betty didn't consult her children. They weren't old enough to work and she being the breadwinner had to decide what was best for them all. This really was an offer too good to refuse. She knew the butcher was stern but she would make sure that no harm would come to her children, as she had a temper when she felt like it.

The children weren't keen on moving into the butcher's house but the thought of eating well helped them to change their minds and accept the inevitable. Their mother was the boss and she had decided. Margaret and her siblings got used to living with another adult, but they never called him dad; he wasn't. The butcher asked them to call him 'Uncle Alf.'

There was rules that 'Uncle Alf' wanted them to abide by and one was that a child had to help him every night after the shop shut. 'That way we can have our tea earlier if I get help to clean up, don't you agree?' he asked. All the kids and Betty agreed. All went well for a few months, until one of the boys went running home crying and into the house, straight into his mum's arms.

'What on earth is the matter, Derek?' she asked.

'Mum, I want to go home to our old house, I don't like helping him in the shop after everyone has gone home, I'm scared of him.'

Betty couldn't believe what she was hearing but Margaret knew very well Uncle Alf had tried it on with her. As she was a strong person she soon put him in his place.

Margaret didn't mention it to her mum as she didn't want to cause trouble. She could see that Uncle Alf was a bully and she was scared for her mother. Of course, Betty believed what Uncle Alf said, that it was just a bit of fun and Derek would get much worse when he went out into the big bad world. The children talked about it amongst themselves and they decided that they would go help Uncle Alf in pairs. That lasted a few weeks but it meant that they had to help in the shop more and so it dwindled to back to one child per night. Things quietened down for a while and Uncle Alf behaved himself. Getting help was better than Betty giving him the eye every night. It didn't last for long as Margaret was turning into a beauty and his mind started thinking 'thoughts.'

Margaret was getting fed up fending Uncle Alf off and he was stronger than her. There was no use saying anything to her mum, as Betty just wouldn't believe her children. She was in a lovely home, she didn't have to go out to work and although she didn't like the bedroom part, she could put up with that compared to what she had when Bob died. She still loved and missed Bob but he was gone and she had to be realistic and for the sake of her children she had to grin and bear it.

One night when Margaret was busy cleaning out the back of the shop she thought she was alone and so she was day-dreaming of what might be for her in the future. She didn't hear Uncle Alf come quietly up behind her, putting one of his hands on her mouth and the other round her waist.

Swiftly he had her down in the sawdust. 'Keep your mouth shut, or you and your mother will be out on the street. Nod if you understand.'

Margaret couldn't do anything else except nod and she knew without a doubt what he was going to do. She was screaming inside when he had his way with her. Silent tears ran down her face. 'Where are you, Dad?' she cried inside. 'Where are you, I need you.'

The great fat butcher climbed off her and said, 'Now Missy Good-shoes, don't you ever tell your mother, cause the minute you do, you will all be out on the street, do you understand? And nobody will believe you if you go to the police, I am well respected in the community.'

Margaret could only nod. She wished that she could die there and then. 'In future, when I want to have you, I shall and if you are good I shall leave the other children alone, do you understand?' Again, Margaret nodded and got up and cleaned herself the best she could. Her mum didn't notice anything different as the butcher made a fuss of Betty for the rest of that night and all week.

The other children noticed that the butcher was nicer to them and they began to enjoy living there and couldn't understand why Margaret was so moody, sulky and bad-tempered all of a sudden.

Margaret put up with the butcher's vicious attacks for as long as she could, until she could no longer put her family first. Her mind was going to explode if she didn't do something about it and although she wanted to murder him she knew that that wasn't the way out for her. The only thing she could do was run away. A twelve-year-old girl running away? Where could she go?

Anywhere but here. She didn't tell anyone what she was going to do. She simply left a note to her mum to say that she was going away but that she was okay.

Margaret left one morning to go to school but instead went to the bus station to see where the furthest bus would take her. She had the pocket money the butcher had given all the children for the chores they did. Although Margaret did more than any of her siblings, she didn't get more than them. She saved every penny to take her far, far away from that evil person.

She bought a ticket for London, determined to enjoy the journey and think about the consequences when she arrived at her destination. She had taken plenty of food with her she could have a little feast on the bus. Margaret had a seat all to herself and was fascinated by the scenery. They had never gone on holiday, so she was making up for lost time. Crikey knew what was in store for her in The Smoke as they called London.

The bus travelled all night, picking up passengers at many depots, but Margaret was lucky as no one sat beside her. She got talking to a man who was going to London and when he asked her why she was travelling on her own, she said she was going to be picked up by an aunty in London. That seemed to satisfy the man for he didn't bother her anymore. She managed to get some sleep and before she knew it they were there. Now what was she going to do?

'Oh, no, what have I done?' Margaret said aloud.

The man she was speaking to on the bus came up behind her and said, 'What is the matter, young lady? I thought your aunty was picking you up?'

'Oh, yes, yes, she is, she was, well, I thought she was but now I'm not sure.' Margaret was making a hash of speaking and not knowing what she was saying. 'Oh, I don't know, I really don't know what I am doing.'

The man asked kindly, 'Have you run away from home?' When Margaret nodded, he said 'Okey dokey, let's go into that cafe and get you some breakfast.'

'Thank you, but I don't know you and you aren't going to send me home. I am not going back to that horrid man.'

'Calm down, calm down, I'm not going to send you home. If you want I can take you to stay with my aunt Madge, she helps girls and boys who run away and they all love her,' the man said soothingly. Margaret wasn't sure, but she was so hungry and anything was better than being at home. Reluctantly she followed the man.

'Hey, I don't even know your name.'

'My name is Tony, okay? And what is yours?' he said cheekily with a smile.

'My name is Margaret, and I am so hungry, can we please go to your Aunty Madge?'

The man started hurrying away, shouting, 'Okay, then but we'll have to run to catch the local bus.' Margaret ran faster than the man and got on the bus before him but she let him pay as she didn't know where they were going.

In no time at all they reached their destination and arrived at aunty Madge's door ravishing. After knocking at the door, Tony walked in, shouting, 'Aunty Madge, it's Tony here, are you home?'

The voice from the kitchen shouted, 'Of course I am, come on through if your feet's clean,' and she gave a loud bellow of a laugh. 'My, what have we here?' she said when she saw Margaret.

'This is Margaret and she is so hungry that she could eat a horse, do you happen to have one, Aunty? Ha, ha, ha.'

Margaret liked the look of Aunty Madge; she was old but with a cheery face and even though she had a cigarette hanging out of her mouth, Margaret just knew she was here forever.

It looked as if Aunty Madge had taken a liking to Margaret too. They exchanged look, appearing to have a secret only they both knew about each other. They were cemented for life. Aunty Madge had a council house but she gave Margaret a room to herself as she said she was a growing girl and needed her privacy. The other people living in the house were Aunty Madge's five sons aged between eleven and seventeen, and they had to share one room. Aunty Madge was giving them orders before they hurried out of the house with parcels under their arms.

It didn't take long for Margaret to settle down and though she ached for her family, she knew that she could never ever go back; and here, she knew she was safe.

It appeared that Aunty Madge had her own business that she ran from the house. Whenever Margaret walked into the kitchen, the conversation changed to another subject.

'Aunty Madge, why do you always stop speaking when I walk into the room when you have visitors?' she asked one day.

'Well, dearie, you are such a lovely girl that I don't want you to get involved in wrong doings and that is what I have been doing for many years. I don't want to see you get hurt,' she whispered.

'Aunty Madge, you saved my life and I will always be in your debt and I just know that you could never do anything bad as you have been so good to me.'

Tony was there that day and he gave a sly smile to Aunty Madge, aware that today would be the end or the start of a new turn in Margaret's life. What would Aunty Madge do?

Aunty Madge tried to explain to Margaret, that the only way she knew how to make a living was to help a friend sell wares that other people wanted. As she had been doing it for years, she found it very hard to stop and she didn't want Margaret getting mixed up in it.

'Aunty Madge, I said you have saved my life, now I want to pay you back by helping you, please, I know you are not a horrid person, please let me help you.'

Aunty Madge and Tony looked at each other, as they had been friends for years they could read each others eyes and after a few minutes, they both nodded.

'All right, young lady, now sit down and I shall tell you what I do and if you don't like it we shall say no more about it and if you want to move out, we shall find you a room somewhere so you can start afresh, okay?'

Margaret nodded as she sat on the high-backed chair beside the table and was intrigued at the mystery of it all. Once Margaret had been told what the mystery was, she got up off the chair, went out the kitchen door and up to her room where she sat for many hours, thinking and thinking and thinking.

Aunty Madge and Tony left her to it as she had to make up her own mind what she wanted to do. After about four hours, Margaret came back into the kitchen where Aunty Madge and Tony still were, and she announced, 'I'm in.'

Weeks passed into months and months passed into years and the business that Aunty Madge started was flourishing due to Margaret's foresight. Margaret never touched any of the merchandise and for that matter neither did Aunty Madge as they both wanted and needed clear heads. The empire grew and where once Aunty Madge's name was held in awe, it was now Margaret's, as she had the aura, the presence, the style and good communication with the Big Boys.

Nobody tried to muscle in on their patch and anyone trying to do so knew the consequences as Aunty Madge's five sons were now well-known 'minders'. Although they never went looking for trouble, everyone knew not to cross them.

Margaret thought less and less about her mum and family. In time she didn't think about them at all, as there was no point in going back to them. She had made a new life for herself and she even married Aunty Madge's eldest son Jason. Even though they didn't have children they were as happy as any other couple.

Until one day.

It started the same as any other morning. They still lived in the same house but three of the sons had moved out to a new apartment. The radio was up loud as usual, with the music and singing belting out for all to hear, when the doorbell rang. They could hardly hear the bell for the noise of the radio until someone turned it down.

'Someone's at the door,' Jason yelled to whoever was within earshot and it just so happened it was Margaret that was nearest. As she opened the door, the police charged in, nearly knocking her over.

'What is going on here? You can't barge in here without a warrant, get out!'

'Sorry, Mrs M but we do have a warrant. Jason Mason, I am arresting you for the possession of twenty kilos of heroin.'

At that point, Margaret collapsed and by the time she came to, Jason had been taken away by the police.

The doorbell brought Margaret back to the present time and she chuckled as she said to herself, 'No, this is certainly not *Coronation Street,* and that must be Alex at the door.'

Alex didn't know that Margaret had already sussed him out. She had to pretend that she didn't know anything about him so invited him over to get to know him better. Margaret had got one of her heavies to break into Alex's house and go through his things, but nothing was found – he was clean.

After Alex had gone and Margaret was satisfied that he was trustworthy, not that he would know what was in the parcels, but she still had to check him out, she decided to ring Jason as soon as possible. Her helpers were decreasing, either by way of getting caught and sent to prison, or high-tailing it out of the country before being caught. She made sure that she was always safe and never got involved socially with any of the big boys.

'Where have all the years gone?' Margaret asked herself. 'I made Aunty Madge's empire bigger than anyone else in London and now, what have I left? Practically nothing. I must get in touch with Jason cause I can't ask Alex to do deliveries or pick ups for long as he might get suspicious. I'll ring him now.'

Jason was Aunty Madge's eldest son and he and Margaret had been married, but he had been to prison so often that she wanted to keep a wide berth from him. So far the police had never bothered her as she had a respectable hair-dressing salon which was a front for the drugs. Jason was only too pleased to help as he was strapped for cash – because of his police record, all the dealers felt like Margaret and gave him a wide berth, but Margaret was desperate and Jason had been straight for a couple of years now. Jason was going to visit Margaret when it got dark. That way, he could see if anyone was following him; yes he was good at that.

Margaret had a lovely house which she decorated herself as she had a flair for interior design. She could have chosen that road to take but by the time she discovered she had a talent for design, she was well and truly embroiled in the drug business. She liked the neighbours in the street but one wrong word or move and her life, her good life could come crashing down – and she had worked too long and hard for that to happen.

She didn't feel guilty about selling drugs to innocent juveniles or rich businessmen. She had had a raw deal from the butcher and thought that it was 'eat or be eaten' in this world. Margaret didn't think she was all bad. She gave thousands to the children's hospitals and at Christmas time she found out who was alone at Christmas and every year had donated huge food parcels to down-and-out pensioners. No she didn't think she was wholly bad, but she was alone in that opinion.

When Jason arrived after dark, he was leaner than the last time she had seen him and her heart gave a little flutter before she checked herself. *No, not with him again, I couldn't trust him. Then what am I doing with him now?* Because he was older, and she didn't have anyone else she could trust, and Aunty Madge had passed away five years previously.

She explained to Jason what she wanted him to do, just pick up the big parcels and deliver them to her after dark, that way no one would see him, and to deliver the made-up parcels after dark too. She would get Stuart and Alex to deliver small packets, that way they wouldn't be suspicious. Yes, Margaret was sure that would work, as long as Jason kept his hands to himself and didn't go dipping in the merchandise, she would give him a trial. It was good to see Jason again but there was no going back to getting hitched with him again. When Margaret went to bed alone that night she felt better. She even thought she would maybe start to paint her hall to brighten the place up. With Tom doing the garden for her she felt that everything was going to work out.

Alex had been working for Margaret for a few months now and he had turned out to be reliable to the extent that she had got him to deliver some large parcels when Jason was otherwise engaged. Margaret still didn't want Alex to do too much. She had already given him more work than she had intended, due to Jason. She knew Alex wasn't 'one of her kind' and had to tread carefully when speaking to him as she might let slip some confidential information.

Alex was so considerate, genuine, helpful, eager to please, just to get into Margaret's 'circle' that she had to hold back many times and treat him like a neighbour doing a few errands for her. She didn't want him involved totally with what she was doing as she was the 'Queen pin' and nobody else ran this business but her, but at the same time it was getting too much for her. She seriously thought of giving it up but couldn't find anyone to pass the business over to. Jason couldn't be trusted as he didn't have a brain in his head and the rest of the family had been in and out of prison so many times that it was like going to Butlin's holiday camp for them. No, of all the people that she knew and had worked with over the years there was very few trustworthy, intelligent, far-seeing men who could run and operate such a stealthy lucrative business that she had built up.

Margaret would have to do some serious thinking about the future if she was hoping to give up the business soon. She felt her luck had lasted longer than it should have, considering the near misses that she'd had. Changing her name and moving to different parts of the country many times was all part and parcel of the game and she hadn't minded it for the first few years. But now she liked this town and wanted to be a respectable citizen, able to join committees and have her face show in the papers, which she couldn't have had during all those years.

She could have stayed in London heading Aunty Madge's empire, but Margaret had her eyes on the bigger picture and she ended up getting too big for her boots. That worked well for a few years but when new gangs tried to muscle into her patch she lost a few good men trying to keep hold of a bigger patch than she really needed.

One of her heavies, who had a head on his shoulders, had said, 'Margaret, you have more than you need and can handle, why not go into partnership with the Manner gang? You would have better protection for your helpers which is a much needed thing in this day and age and also, maybe even grow bigger.'

Margaret got angry, having someone tell her what to do was sacrilege, even coming from Tommy, who had been with Aunty Madge for years was no excuse. She turfed him out, while knowing that what he said had a rather larger grain of truth than she cared to admit.

The Manner gang were tired of waiting for an answer from Margaret and one night when there was a larger than normal delivery of drugs at a disused factory in the east end they struck. The deliveries were always at different places and only the need to know were informed at the last minute, so how the Manner gang got to know of the exchange, Margaret was never able to find out but she always thought that it was Tommy, as she used the same sequence and he was one of the few who knew how she operated. Even though she used different places every time, it wouldn't have taken Tommy long to calculate the site for that night.

She lost good men that night and all the deliveries for the next month. She didn't believe in guns but the Manner gang thought differently and Margaret knew then that they were too big for her. She didn't want to lose any more good men, so one night she high-tailed it out of London, never to return. She didn't get in touch with her 'family' as she called them, for over a year and only when she knew it was safe to do so. Through one or two trustworthy relatives, Margaret and Aunty Madge were able to keep up a correspondence by mail passed from one person to another and so forth until no one could possible track down where Margaret was living. The sad part for Margaret, was that she couldn't attend Aunty Madge's funeral and didn't even know about it until three weeks after the event due to the process of the letters.

Although it would be safe to go back to London, Margaret felt that the further away from there the better and the only good thing there had gone, Aunty Madge, so there was no point in going back. Jason and her were in contact and that was enough.

Jason had dropped off a big parcel three nights before and Margaret had divided the goods into many different smaller packages to go to her clients. She rang Jason to say that they were ready for him to deliver. She didn't like the drugs in her house for longer than necessary and started to get twitchy when Jason didn't answer his phone.

Up to now, he had been reliable and this was out of character, he would always tell her what he was going to do after he delivered the parcel to let her know where he would be when she was ready to contact him for deliveries. He had said that he was going back to his house to do some painting then gardening so he would be ready for when she rang. She tried a few times during the rest of the day but still no answer. She didn't know what she was going to do, so she tried to concentrate on finishing the packaging and even shredding some vital addresses.

Margaret loved knitting as it helped her relax. She sat in her favourite armchair in the lounge and got her pattern book out. *Maybe if I start that jumper that I was going to do for Jason, it might take my mind off things until he rings.*

That didn't last long as she couldn't concentrate and soon found herself having cups of tea, the odd cigarette and even a glass of whisky. Nothing was making the time pass, it was getting darker and the street lights were on, so Margaret closed the curtains and took another cigarette, not going outside to smoke it as she usually, did – she was past caring.

She did a lot of pacing back and forth on the lounge carpet. It would have taken a lot of friction to make a hole in the carpet as it was the very best that money could buy, so Margaret could pace all night if she wanted. Of course she didn't 'want', what she wanted was Jason to answer his bloody phone, the drugs had to be delivered tomorrow and she had an uneasy feeling about asking Alex to deliver such a huge amount.

The doorbell rang, 'Thank goodness, at last, Jason, just wait till I get a hold of him, I think it really is time to retire.' Margaret was so relieved that she was nearly crying, the stress of the day had finally taken over, she was too old for this business, far too old. She heard a commotion outside the door and wondered if Jason had brought someone with him. It wouldn't have surprised her if he had, although she had told him sternly that under no circumstance was he to bring anyone here and up to now he hadn't. Margaret opened the door and found Alex standing there.

'Why, Alex, what …' that was all that she was able to say.

Alex said, 'Margaret Shore, alias, Bentley, I have a warrant to search this premises as I believe there may be drugs which are in your possession and that you are in the process of selling them.'

Stunned speechless, Margaret nearly fainted. She collapsed against the wall. Was she dreaming? This had to be a nightmare! This was not happening, not to her, Margaret! There had to be some mistake, she had been careful, she was always so careful!

'Margaret Shore, alias Bentley, do you wish to have a solicitor present while we search your house?' Alex spoke to Margaret with authority but with a tinge of sadness as he had really liked her as a person. Then he thought of all the lives that she had helped destroy with her drugs and so pushed the sadness to the back of his mind. She didn't need sympathy.

At the same time that he was thinking that, Margaret was thinking, Alex! her neighbour! her courier! Alex who she very nearly considered handing over her empire to! Alex! Alex her neighbour, who was standing at her door with uniformed police behind him. Alex! This must be a joke, but no, it couldn't be. Because she did have drugs in her house, Jason wasn't here and how could Alex know? None of it added up – but of course it added up, her luck had well and truly run dry. How had it happened? She had been very careful, all those years she had gone over, checked everything twice, sometimes three times.

Alex was speaking to her, but she hadn't heard him as other police officers were rushing into the house, searching in all the rooms for the magic parcels which were easy enough to find. Margaret felt after all the years she had been in the house that she didn't need to hide the parcels before they were taken to her clients, well it didn't matter now, it was too late she had slipped up somewhere, too late.

Margaret did indeed phone a solicitor that was above corruption and one which she had used regularly and he was, to say the least, stunned when he got her call and even speechless when he eventually arrived at her house to see so many policemen there.

Mr Wheatly soon became professional after the initial shock and got down to business saying that he would represent Margaret. He wandered round the house with Alex listening to all he had to say about the 'sting' and Alex was helpful in putting Raymond in the picture but kept everything professional and not telling him that he was Margaret's neighbour, that would come later. Before they took Margaret away to the police station to charge her she asked Alex if she could have a few minutes alone with him.

'I'm sorry Margaret, I'm afraid those days are gone, but you can speak to me with your solicitor present.'

Margaret desperately wanted to know how she was caught after all the trouble she took to remain invisible, so she asked Alex that question in front of Raymond. 'Well, it can't do any harm telling you now, Margaret, but you were televised at the Edinburgh Military Tattoo, one of the three night that they do recording and one of your previous associates in London who was watching the program spotted you. We have spent the last few years searching for you and when we found you, I went under cover to become your neighbour. I knew it was you that searched my house before asking me to deliver your parcels, so I was forewarned.'

'Oh no, the one time that I thought it was safe to mingle in a crowd, I suppose you have got hold of Jason too?'

'Yes, Margaret, glad to say, we do and also glad to say that your empire has crumbled, at last,' said Alex as he led Margaret out of her house.

Margaret was screaming inside herself. She loved this house, she loved the time she had spent in the street, with most of the neighbours being beaut and most of all, she had really liked Alex. How the mighty had fallen. She should have given up selling drugs before she moved into the house, but then she would never have met Alex and it was all meant to be.

Her time was finished. When she was sitting in a lonely cell in prison she might think about all the lives she had helped destroy, but at the moment, all she could thing about was herself, Margaret.

Before they went out of the gate, Margaret turned to Alex and said. 'Alex, could I ask you one last favour please? Could you ask Tom to keep looking after my garden for me?'

Number 6 Glenfield Court

Alex Craig lived at number six Glenfield Court and had done for two years. He had moved there from his home town six hours drive away. He had won some money in the pools, which let him get completely away after his divorce. He had thought she was the love of his life, but now he wanted to be as far away from her as possible. He felt free to go as far as he wanted since they had no children.

He didn't want to dwell on his first marriage or see her around the haunts they had both frequented for most of their lives. They had known each other nearly all their lives and his friends were her friends and vice versa, so it was better to cut the cord and make a new start and a new life.

He went looking on the net for property in certain areas in towns near the sea, and it didn't take him long to locate just the spot that he wanted. He went looking at a few in the town but when he came upon the bungalow in Glenfield Court, he just knew that it was the one. It was a real find and the couple who were selling were moving into a granny flat that their daughter had built onto the side of her large house.

As Alex had won a substantial amount, he decided to give up work for a couple of years or until he felt he wanted to get back to the workforce. So far he was enjoying the free life and had spent most of the last two years renovating, decorating and make number six a home. He also liked to go hill running and cycling, so he spent a lot of time in the first three months in his new abode, doing just that. The hills were just at the outskirts of the town, so easy to get to without using his motor bike. He would go up to the hills two to three times a week and met people that he had seen often before, all with the same thought as him. Everyone had a different reason for running in the hills and Alex often wondered about the other people's reasons.

Alex liked to observe people and work out how they worked, he was a good people-watcher and had taken a course in it at night school, the wonders of finding out about people and their habits, amazing! In the meantime, Alex enjoyed his time in the hills on his own with his thoughts and dreams of the future.

Running, to feel the wind in his face, to push himself as much as he could, as if trying to get rid of the past, to push it as far away as his mind threw it. The scenery on top of the hills was breathtaking and Alex would sit there for hours scanning the view of the town and surrounding area. He always took his high-powered binoculars with him to home in on certain places to get a better look.

Yes the view from the hills was certainly an eye-opener. Although he didn't dwell on one particular view he accidentally espied a lady lying on a sun bed in her back yard – naked! Alex quickly turned away to another view almost as if the lady had caught him which she wouldn't have but he was so embarrassed that he gave up viewing for a while. He didn't want to be a peeping tom.

Alex was in his thirties, tall, handsome and with fair hair and even though all the girls swooned whenever they saw him, he was now going steady with Chloe who he had met at the bowling alley eighteen months ago.

Chloe was in her thirties and had never married as she had concentrated on her career and had lived in South Africa for a few years working with people in remote villages. She had loved being there but had to come back home after five years due to unrest in the country. Alex had asked Chloe to move in with him about six months before and things were going well, one reason maybe, being, that as Chloe was a nurse, worked shifts, loved her job and had no intentions of giving it up, he knew that she wouldn't get under his feet all the time. He needed lots of time to himself as he was working on a project and couldn't be disturbed. Chloe had a large family so she caught up with them during her time off, so all in all their relationship was working out just fine.

Alex loved being with Chloe, but he wanted to make sure that this was the one before actually proposing. He had been burnt once and it wasn't going to happen again, being married to Eileen was good for a while until she decided that she didn't want to be married anymore as she had taken a liking to the other gender. Alex couldn't fight that and so he wanted to make sure this time, although after telling Chloe about his first marriage, she said that she had no inkling to 'go there' so he was safe with her in that point.

Yes, everything seemed to be going well with Alex and Chloe.

In his other life he had worked in the public service and winning the money meant he could pick and choose when he wanted to get back to work. He had made up some flyers and put them into people's letter boxes letting them know that if they wanted any handy work done, he was their man! Alex didn't want to do a lot of handy work and this way, he could decide, if and when. Up to now he had got a couple of replies from neighbours and had put up photo frames, fixed a couple of gates and run about on his motorbike picking up and delivering parcels, which was cheaper than posting them. As with the majority of the residents in the court, he wasn't one for gardening and appreciated it when Tom asked if he would like him to do his. Tom did a good job and allowed Alex to pick which plants he wanted but Tom always gave him advice about the best ones. Yes, on the whole, life in Glenfield Court was good and he was glad he had made the move here.

There was one niggling thing that had happened recently but he hadn't mentioned it to Chloe as he didn't want to alarm her. Alex had been a very meticulous person from a very early age, beginning when he was in the Boy Scouts and carried on right up to the present. The training he had received in the Scouts had been good grounding which had helped him all through his life so far.

If he had put something down on a bench and it had been moved even a fraction, he knew someone had touched or read it. Even when he was at work and someone moved his pen or book, he knew and he liked being like that. It wasn't a phobia, just his being careful about things. He had not told Chloe as he didn't want her to think that he was some sort of freak, which he wasn't and it didn't affect their relationship in any way. The niggling thing that Alex noticed was that someone other than Chloe and him had been in his house, they hadn't been invited and they didn't come in by the front door neither, he could stake his life on that. On the ground at the back door, there was a mat for wiping muddy feet, and Alex noticed that it wasn't square on as it usually was. Although he didn't put too much heed on that, on the other hand the mat on the inside had definitely been moved and it wasn't done by Chloe or himself. He remembered before they had gone out, he had checked that the back door was locked and had scanned the room as he always did before leaving.

One thing he had asked Chloe to do was make sure that all doors were shut whenever they left the house. The reason he gave was so that in the event of a fire, the fire could be contained in the one room until the fire brigade arrived, another reason he gave was that by keeping the doors closed it kept the heat in and Chloe had agreed as her parents had always instilled in their children about closing doors behind them, ever since she was young. So no problem there!

As it happened, Alex was the last person to leave the house that day and of course all the doors had been closed, but when he had got home before Chloe one door leading to his office was open. That intrigued him, so he opened the door wider and without stepping inside, scanned his beady eyes around the room looking to see if anything was out of place.

The first thing he noticed was that his waste paper basket wasn't in its usual spot. He always kept it to the right of his computer, and it was now beside his chair. Anyone else wouldn't have noticed but with Alex's trained eye, no detail was missed. The mouse at his computer was facing a different way to the way he always left it when he was finished with it.

The mail that he had to the left of his desk was now in the centre and books on his bookshelf had been taken out and put back differently, ever so slightly but to Alex's eyes, very noticeable.

Well, well, well, I wonder who that could have been, he thought. Alex walked around his house checking other points of interest and saw that they had been in his wardrobe, his dressing table, under his bed and his suitcase. They were professional but not professional enough as they didn't know what they were up against when it came to Alex's expertise! Some pictures on the walls were slightly out of kilter and Alex tut-tutted at the sloppy attitude they had to other peoples belongings. He knew that they wouldn't be back, as they had come for one purpose only,- and didn't find anything to steal.

'They, whoever they are, have been thorough, but there is nothing to pinch this time,' he said aloud. He knew the reason they had entered his house and gone through his things but he had to keep that to himself.

Nothing had been stolen as he didn't keep money or valuables in his house. It didn't look as if Chloe's personal belongings were touched after having a quick look in her wardrobe and cupboards.

Alex decided not to mention any of this to Chloe, as really there was nothing to tell her, nothing was stolen or wrecked and he was pretty sure they wouldn't be back, so better to keep quiet and not worry her.

Alex was correct. For the next few months, no unwelcome visitors came to their house when they weren't in and so he settled down to just waiting. Life went along the same as usual for Alex and Chloe and they even managed a weekend away to France as it didn't take long to fly to the continent as there was an airport in the next city. They both loved the French cuisine and they found they had even more in common than they first thought; yes, life was going along nicely for the two of them. The walk along the banks of the Seine was special for them and they agreed to go back the same time next year for they both knew that their time there was an omen for a happy future together.

One morning the phone rang in the middle of Alex's day-dreaming about another holiday that this time, he was going to surprise Chloe. 'Hello,' he said brightly, as Alex always had a good telephone manner.

'Hello, Alex, it is Margaret from next door. Are you busy or could you come in for a coffee? I would like to speak to you, please.'

Alex thought, aha, this is one for the books. 'Sure, Margaret, I shall come over right away, if that is okay with you?'

Margaret said, 'Yes, that would be great, see you in a minute.'

'Um, I wonder what she wants. I have delivered a few parcels for her and collected some too but she has never invited me into her house.' Alex spoke aloud to himself – or to someone that he couldn't see?

After giving his face a wash and putting on some nice deodorant, he made his way out his door, down the path with lovely colourful flowers that Tom had planted on either side, opened the gate, shut the gate and walked purposely next door to Margaret's house, knowing that he would have been watched.

Alex was just about to knock on the door again when it opened by itself, or rather by Margaret who was standing behind it. 'Come in, Alex, come on in, how are you today?'

'Thanks, Margaret, yes, I am well and you?'

'I too am fine thank you, now would you like a coffee or a tea?'

'Coffee would suit me fine, thanks, Margaret.' They went into the kitchen and Margaret made the coffee, picked up some biscuits and they went into the lounge as it was nicer there. Alex's lounge was bare compared to Margaret's, but she was a lot older than him so had many more years to accumulate fancies and one could see she had matched everything to perfection.

Margaret asked Alex about himself and he felt he was being interviewed for a job that he hadn't applied for. He let her go on as he didn't have anything to hide and what he didn't want people to know he simply made something up. Weren't women good at that, he thought. If they could do it, so could he; anyway nobody was getting hurt.

Margaret went on to explain that she needed a good driver to collect parcels and deliver them, just what he had been doing on the odd occasion for her, but now she wanted to know if he wanted the job on a permanent basis. 'You, see, I have a small business I run from home and I buy goods wholesale and sell them retail to customers I have had for years. You know the kind of thing, facials, body lotions, bubble bath, shampoos, all nice smelly stuff. One of my couriers, who I used a lot, has had a bad accident and won't be able to continue helping me for a long time. I need someone I can trust and as I have used you occasionally over the past couple of years, I was wondering if you would help me out. You wouldn't have to collect any money as the retailers put the money straight into my bank account.'

Margaret went on to explain everything that Alex would need to know. It sounded just the job for him as it wasn't every day and only a couple of hours every other day and it would mean that he could still concentrate on his 'project.' Alex said that he couldn't think of any problem that would deter him from doing it and it would be nice to get out and about meeting different people.

They talked some more about conditions, money and how heavy the parcels would be, as Alex's only transport was a motorbike. Margaret said she didn't see a problem with that as it was small parcels and they wouldn't be more than he could handle.

'Thanks, Margaret, that seems ideal for me. I don't want a full time job as I am going to be doing some studying so part time suits me fine.'

Alex knew that Margaret would ask what he was going to be studying so he had an answer already thought up, he didn't want everyone knowing his business so he always had back up reasons and lies at the ready. 'I thought I would like to study nursing, they are always crying out for medical staff and I am not too old to try. I plan to study only part time for a year with the occasional shift weekly, so wish me luck, ha, ha.'

'I certainly do, Alex that is a great profession and I wish you all the best.'

Margaret stood up and they both went towards the front door before she said, 'If you don't mind, Alex, could you do a delivery tomorrow evening about six o'clock, as the customer works during the day and doesn't get home until then, if you find it an inconvenience any time just let me know and I can change the time, okay?'

'Thanks Margaret, that sounds great and I am sure there won't be any problem, bye for now.'

'Goodbye, Alex and thanks once again, see you tomorrow,' and with that she closed the door behind him and got on with whatever she was doing before she had rang Alex.

'Well, well, well, things are looking up, I am glad I found this house and moved into it, I wonder what is going to happen next, this is my lucky day.'

As usual, Alex was speaking to himself and thought he had better stop doing that as one didn't know if one was being listened to. With that he went out to his shed and rang someone on his mobile. Even on the phone, anyone listening into his mobile would think he was speaking to a friend or relative as the conversation was very bland. When he came out of the shed, he made sure he had a spade in his hand to use so that he gave the impression that he was going to do some gardening, then pretended to answer his mobile.

All that performance was in the event that he might be being watched, he couldn't afford to take any chances, now, when he had come so far. Tonight, they would celebrate, he would take Chloe out for a lovely meal, the excuse being that he had got a part time job, that was better than nothing, a start, a positive start in the right direction.

Alex two months on.

The night was cool with a wind starting to get up and no sign of the rain, the gardens needed. There were stars in the sky like diamonds sitting on a black velvet cushion with the moon watching over them. The lights in the big building in the centre of town were on in every room and it was lit up like a Christmas tree making the surrounding area like a beacon for anyone who had lost their way or were looking to be locked up!

It wasn't the usual evening shift that was on duty at Police Headquarters this particular night but a specialised team dealing in drug raids. This was overtime for the officers who had volunteered – it wasn't every night that there were raids. As the officers spoke amongst themselves the door opened with such force that they knew who was about to enter the room.

The Superintendent strode into the office like a whirlwind, seeing ten officers sitting at their desks or standing waiting for the instructions which were about to be forthcoming. The Super was a big man, nearly six foot, a bit on the tubby side but he kept fit by lots of walking, running and hiking, oh yes, no one crossed the Super!

The officers knew they were going out on a night raid but other than that it was a case of a need to know basis. That was part of the job and they all knew it and were prepared to accept it as such, as all the officers enjoyed their job. One in particular was Detective Senior Sergeant Alex Craig, who had been doing undercover work for the past two years. Alex wasn't connected to this particular police station but had been seconded due to the fact that the person of interest was living in the town. Only the Super knew about Alex during the past two years as secrecy about the assignment was top priority. They would communicate by phone and the odd time when both of them went walking or running up in the hills making sure beforehand that there was no one that would see them together. Espionage at its best!!

'All right men, just stay where you are or get a seat if you need, we are about to tell you about the drug raid that is going down tonight.' The Super who had been carrying papers put them down on a table and went through them while everyone got seated or was ready to listen. 'Right men, as you may well have noticed, we have a stranger in our midst. Let me introduce you to Detective Senior Sergeant Alex Craig from Addington Police Headquarters.

Alex has been undercover for the last two years and tonight it will all come to fruition, his hard work will have paid off. Do you want to say something to the men, Alex?'

'Yes, thank you, Chief Superintendent. Hello officers, well tonight is going to be the end of a long undercover stint which hopefully will have paid off. Tonight's raid will not be dangerous, just complete surprise for the person of interest. Although I am quite sure there are no firearms in the house we will of course be wearing our vests even though there will be only one person in the house.

'I have had the house under surveillance for two years now and not many people have visited. The subject has been hiding from the police for many years, so not many people knew where the subject was living. It was quite by chance that the subject was spotted by one of her victims and he reported seeing her, so although it still took us a while to find out where she was living we were helped big time by that information. We have been searching for the subject for years as she went underground for a time.

'There will be a large stash of drugs which will have been divided into small bundles for delivery so they will be easy to find; but there could be more as I don't know if she has a safe or secret places in the house or out back. That is where the dog handler will be great, thanks for that,' as he acknowledged Bruce the dog handler.

Alex looked at the Super not knowing if he wanted him to mention that he was living next door to the subject. 'Anything else you want me to mention, Super?'

The Super got off his chair. 'No thanks Alex, you have said all that is needed, so, men, any question for Alex or me? As Alex said, it isn't going to be a dangerous raid as it will be a surprise with only one person, a woman in the house. No dogs, Alex?'

Alex shook his head, 'No dogs and no cats, sir.'

'Right then, as there are no questions. The time is now eight o'clock. We leave in fifteen minutes and don't make too much noise when we get there as we don't want to alarm the neighbours too much. We shall be walking up to the door of the house and Alex will ring the bell, speak to the subject and we will go in in an orderly fashion.We know that there is only one person in the house just now as a fellow officer has been keeping an eye on the house for the past few days, taking over from Alex when he went out. I have just spoken to him and no one has been to the house today.'

Alex had told everyone in the street that he spoke to, that his cousin from Edinburgh was going to be staying with him for a couple of weeks so if they saw a stranger walking about they would know who it was. When all the officers stood up and put their vests on and got ready to go, Alex was feeling a bit hollow, all his undercover work was going to finish tonight, his 'other life' would be no more, he felt as if he was on the edge of a cliff, but then he brought himself up, he had found Chloe. Chloe who he loved and was going to ask a very important question when he saw her. But wait, this wasn't time to be thinking about love, he had a job to finish and by golly he was going to finish it, it would be sad, but needed to be done and he was going to put everything into it. And with that he too put his vest on and walked towards the door going out into that starry, starry night.

A few weeks beforehand

Alex had asked Chloe, when he knew she had a few days off work, if she minded going to stay with her family. The reason he gave was that he wanted to do some renovation in the house and it was going to be messy with lots of dust flying about. Alex didn't want Chloe to get dust on her and to fall over tools, well that is the explanation that he gave her. As Chloe trusted Alex, she was going to offer to help but knew that he wouldn't have asked her to go and stay with her family if he wanted her to help him. She was beginning to understand him and wondered, secretly if he was doing it as a surprise for her.

'Okay Alex, but please ring me if you think I can help in any way, promise?' as she gave him a kiss and a cuddle before she left for work. 'Just let me know what days I should have off work, as I can change them if I want.'

'Thank you, my darling Chloe, that would be sweet,' giving her a double kiss and cuddle. 'I will find out today and let you know tonight, see you tonight then.' It had been a busy year for Alex and he hadn't been able to get everything done that he wanted to do. He had wanted to do more reading, go on more weekends away with Chloe to the continent, and definitely go on more runs up to the hills and to take up more gardening to give Tom a help. Chloe was a gem and she didn't mind that the last few months had been busy for Alex and that they hadn't spent as much time with each other as they had done previously.

On one rare night when they had gone out for a meal to a lovely romantic restaurant, which had turned out to be their favourite one, Alex took Chloe's hands and told her his plans. 'I promise you Chloe, that soon, very soon, I shall devote more time with you, in fact I am thinking about going back to my previous job as I am too young to be working part time and miss the routine of getting up at the same time each morning and going to work at the same time every day. I know it might seem humdrum, but I enjoyed it.'

Secretly Chloe was excited, as she had never met any of his friends from his home town as they never went there and the way he had been speaking it seemed that he might want to go back there. And maybe take her? *Oh, I hope so.* She kept herself in check, not showing disappointment that they hadn't spent so much time with each other these past few months. She knew that they were meant for each other and she was determined to hang in there.

'Are you sure, Alex? Honest, I don't mind what you do as long as you enjoy it and that we are together. Don't you like working for Margaret? I thought it was an easy job with plenty of free time for you.'

'She is giving me more and more work. Although I like her, it isn't a steady job with steady hours and that is what I miss, but please don't say anything to Margaret about how I am feeling, I shall tell her in my own time. I am telling you because I want you to know that I know how you are feeling and what you have put up with these past few months, coming and going at all odd hours. Just hang in there for me please and I promise you, you will never regret it.'

Chloe felt goose bumps all over. Boy, did she love this man and she knew he loved her and she was prepared to wait forever for him. Well, not really forever, but the way she was feeling at that moment, she wasn't thinking properly, she was in seventh heaven. The restaurant was warm with a lovely fire burning, it was cosy and dim with romantic music playing from somewhere and there was no one near them to hear what they had to say to each other. 'Alex, I know you are a secret person and I have never intruded and I won't now, I know that you will tell me when you are ready and I am content to wait, for the moment.'

Alex knew that this woman was the one for him, always had been from the first moment that they had met and he wasn't going to lose her. He also noticed that he could trust her and she never gossiped about people at her work or anyone else for that matter. She went to work, to work, not to tittle-tattle; and once this job was finished he would show her how much she meant to him. 'Chloe, I promise you, soon, I shall tell you everything, but not just yet, then we shall be with each other for ever.'

The present

When the three police cars and the dog unit van arrived as silently as they could in Glenfield Court, everyone's curtains were drawn and nobody appeared to have heard the vehicles as there was no twitching at the curtains and no light shining out of opened ones. The cars drew up outside number five and Alex got out first, jumped onto the pavement, opened the gate and hurried up the path. His heart was beating so fast, he was scared for what he was about to do. At times like this he didn't like his job, making friends with someone then having to bust them after befriending them for months or even years on end.

Get a hold of yourself, Alex, lad you knew the score when you took the job on, you are doing a job that the community respects your for, Alex thought in the seconds before he rang the doorbell. He rang the doorbell and waited what seemed like an eternity. Then the door opened and there stood Margaret, his next-door neighbour. Margaret just looked at Alex with shock all over her face when she saw all the police officers standing behind him.

'Why, Alex ... what ...' was all that she was able to say.

Alex said, 'Margaret Shore, alias Bentley, I have a warrant to search this premises as I believe there may be drugs in your possession and that you are in the process of selling them. Do you wish to have a solicitor present while we search your house?' Alex spoke to Margaret with authority but with a tinge of sadness as he had really liked her as a person, then he thought of all the lives that she had helped to destroy with her drugs and so pushed the sadness to the back of his mind. She didn't need sympathy.

On the whole the raid went well, they got all the drugs in the house, the police dog didn't find anything outside and there was a huge amount of cash stashed in a safe behind a painting that Alex had admired. Alex couldn't wait to get home after taking Margaret to the police station and charging her, he just wanted to get out of there, forget about tonight, forget about the deceit necessary to get her.

All he wanted was to think of the future with Chloe. The minute he got home he rang her. A sleepy Chloe answered her mobile. 'Hello? Alex, are you all right? It's after midnight, what has happened?'

'Oh, Chloe, I am sorry to have woken you – no I'm not, I am glad I woke you, because I want you to come home as soon as you can. At first light come home, please, I don't want us to be separated again. I love you, I love you so much, I want you home.'

A stunned Chloe couldn't believe what she was hearing. 'Oh Alex, are you sure you're okay? I love you too and I will come home now, I am on my way, I don't want us to be separated again. I hate being away from you.'

'Chloe, hold on, please stay there until light and when you come home in the morning, I want to ask you a very important question.'

Number 7 Glenfield Court

Chris had been on holiday, enjoying a morning cup of tea and reading the newspaper, when she saw number seven Glenfield Court advertised for sale. The house appealed to her immediately. When she went to inquire about it she was told that an elderly lady, a renowned author, had lived there until her passing quite recently.

'I knew there was something about the house,' Chris told her sister, Anne. 'It was meant for me.'

Chris was five feet nothing, was on the tubby side, and had grey hair which she coloured brown whenever the roots shone through. She was blessed with the weirdest sense of humour any Scot could have. Well, she'd had a weird sense of humour – but that was before the accident.

Her sister asked if she was going to uproot everything to move to the town just because the house had belonged to an author. 'What are you going to do? You can't give up your job at the lawyers, surely?'

'I am going to write. I have always wanted to write and this house is beckoning me to do just that, if I don't do it now, I shall never have the courage to see if I can make it, I just know that this house is telling me to buy it.'

She left her job and home and settled into this adventure with such vigour that at times she scared herself with the zest that she was feeling. She set about decorating the whole house herself. She had painted her old unit so she was well equipped to tackle anything; she was ready and raring to go. So excited was she that sometimes, she forgot to eat, she was on a mission and wanted so badly to start writing. This house had a good feel about it and she was sure Samantha, the elderly lady who had lived in it, was still hovering about. Chris could feel her presence.

She painted every room a different colour. The kitchen was in yellow as Chris thought it was a bright cheery colour to welcome the new dawn. Other rooms were painted blue, green, mauve, lilac. All the colours of the rainbow really, as she wanted to be surrounded by bright cheery colours. Once the decorating was done and everything shipshape, Chris decided to start writing and was very excited about preparing all that needed to be done. She didn't have a special room in which to write; she used many rooms. Depending on her mood when she was writing she would sit in one of the rooms to match her feelings. No one else could understand but then no one else was quite like Chris.

Chris spent the first two years in her home writing many stories, short, long and very long. She knew she had a story in her, it was just waiting for the inspiration to come out of her head.

She hired an agent, Stuart Waters and after reading what she had written to date, he agreed with her that there was the potential for a great novel, just waiting to emerge. She became friends with Stuart and he introduced her to some of his friends at the Jazz Club.

She hadn't had time to go out and meet new people so the first night at the jazz club was very refreshing after being stuck inside her home for months on end with just one thing on her mind. Stuart had many friends and in no time they became Chris's friends too. She often went to the club on her own as she loved jazz.

One night she was introduced to Fiona, a friend of Stuart's who had been working overseas and had just arrived home after two years away.

Fiona was the opposite of Chris, she was tall, slim and dressed in black leather carrying a motorbike helmet, a definite air of confidence about her.

'Chris, this is our friend Fiona, she has been absent for a while, but now she is home to stay and if you ever feel like buddying up with her just a word of warning, she likes fast motorbikes, ha, ha, ha,' said Stuart.

Chris had had a couple of serious boyfriends but none went as far as getting engaged or married. When she met Fiona she felt an unusual stirring inside. She didn't like it – SHE wasn't interested in the other side. *No way* she thought to herself, she felt quite sick and excused herself saying she wasn't feeling well.

Chris's fear kept her away from the club for a couple of weeks. She made the excuse to herself that she really had to write some more stories to get ahead if she was ever going to become an author. 'Oh, my goodness,' Chris said to herself, for the millionth time since she had met Fiona. 'No way, go away, I don't want those feelings, especially about another woman, where on earth does it come from, ah!'

Chris was getting quite upset and the more upset she got the more she thought about Fiona.

One evening when Chris was, as usual, fighting with her mind about what to do, the doorbell rang. Thinking it was Tom about the garden, she opened the door with a smile on her face and looked straight into the eyes of Fiona.

Chris just stood there, stunned, looking at Fiona with her mouth open. Fiona said, 'Hello, Chris, do you mind if I come in? I haven't seen you at the club for a while and I wondered if you were ill or something.

Chris stood like a statue for such a long time that Fiona turned her around and shut the door before steering Chris into the kitchen where she put the kettle on.

Fiona moved into Chris's house the following week, and for the next five years they were as one. No one in the street seemed to mind, everyone accepted them. Even Tom enjoyed speaking to Fiona about flowers and motor bikes, so all was well in heaven, so to speak.

It wasn't long after Fiona moved in that Chris started to write more exciting, adventurous novels and before the year was out she had a best seller. Her first novel was made into a film and Chris felt that she had arrived. Everything good was happening to her and she was grateful.

'Chris, I can't believe the difference in you and I really believe that meeting Fiona was the making of you, eh?' said Stuart as he sat on her kitchen bench. 'Are you happy, because you both look it and you two teaming up with each other was the making of you both, I have never seen Fiona so glowing.'

'Stuart, I never knew that happiness could feel so happy,' laughed Chris. 'I was meant to buy this house and meant to meet Fiona and it is all going according to the plan of the great universe. I am so very grateful, thank you for introducing me to her. But at the time I hated it, the thought of kissing another woman, ugh. Honest, I felt sick for days after meeting her, ha, ha.'

'Yes, Chris, all's well that ends well, but it isn't finished as you have many more books in you, so keep writing and I shall see you next week.'

The next few years flew past with all good things happening and the occasional arguments between Chris and Fiona, but they never broke up or walked out without speaking to one another.

In the time that Chris and Fiona had been living together, Chris had written three best sellers, then all of a sudden the magic evaporated. Nothing would come out of her head.

Chris had been thinking for a while that the magic between her and Fiona was going too. She couldn't quite put her finger on it, but she had noticed that Fiona would have a faraway look in her eyes when Chris watched her, unobserved.

They still did everything together, while drifting apart. It was a slow gradual process – she didn't notice until it was nearly staring her in the face.

'Is everything okay with you, Fiona?' Chris asked one morning. 'You seem so far away, is everything okay at work?'

'Oh, sorry, Chris, no everything is fine at work. I am in the middle of a new project and it's beginning to annoy me, but other than that, no, nothing is wrong.' Fiona smiled and gave Chris a kiss before she went out the door to work.

'Take care, Fiona,' Chris said to her every morning. Chris didn't like motorbikes but had never stopped Fiona riding one as she had the bike before they met and was a careful rider.

They never did sit down and talk about what was happening to them. Maybe if they had done, the accident might never have happened, for Fiona may have concentrated more.

Chris certainly didn't want to hear anything horrid or final from Fiona as she had never been happier in her life, but there was definitely something wrong.

Fiona was scared to tell Chris what she was feeling. She didn't want to hurt Chris but she couldn't go on the way she was going as it wasn't fair to either of them, but the honest conversation never occurred.

One rainy morning Chris and Fiona had had a silly tiff and Fiona stomped out, late for work. They were always quarrelling but they usually made it up before Fiona went out the door, but this day they didn't.

That day there had been drizzle and the roads were all greasy from the oil of the traffic. Usually Fiona took care but as she was still mulling over the tiff, she didn't concentrate and slid on a patch of oil and went crashing into a stone wall.

She never recovered and neither had Chris. Chris had never forgiven herself for shouting at Fiona. 'If only I hadn't said those awful things,' Chris would say over and over again. No amount of talking by Stuart and the rest of her friends would change her mind, she would have to just go through the anguish until the pain eventually subsided.

That was over a year ago. Under ordinary circumstances, her agent, Stuart would be hounding her more than he had done but because of the tragic accident he kept his distance as much as he could. Stuart knew that Chris had another best seller in her and it was only a matter of time before she would explode it upon the world. In the meantime, Stuart was patient and encouraged her as much as he could, sending meditation tapes with soothing music, the sound of the sea and the rustle of the wind in the forest.

Unknown to Stuart, Chris threw every one in the bin. 'What does he think I am, a machine? Feelings can't be turned on like a switch, or by the sound of the sea, or the seagulls screeching at the fishing boats. I will recover when I am ready, when God thinks me fit, when I think I am fit, not when HE thinks.' And with that, Chris took another drink of dry red wine. There was no time like now for a drink, she thought.

Stuart was getting uneasy as it had been over a year now and still Chris hadn't put pen to paper. Stuart rang Chris's sister Anne 'She simply must start writing again, Anne. This isn't doing her any good. do you see how she drinks, every day?'

'Yes, I know, Stuart. I thought that she would be coming back to the Chris that we all knew; something will have to be done, but I don't know what – she just bites my head off if I mention anything about her drinking.'

'I know it's up to her if she writes again or doesn't,' said Stuart, 'but I am concerned about her health and unless something is done soon she will end up too far gone.'

'Okay, Stuart, leave it to me. I'll talk it over with Richard and see if we can come up with something.'

Even Tom could see all the empty wine bottles in the bin when he did Chris's garden. He didn't want to broach the subject as it wasn't his business but he could see that Chris hadn't got back to her old self since the accident. He wondered what he could do to help. Tom mentioned it to his wife Mary as she was good to discuss problems with, and all she said was, 'She will come out of it in her own good time.'

Tom didn't agree. Chris appeared to be slipping further away all the time and soon she would be out of reach. He must think what he could do. Tom had his own problems but he liked this street he lived in, he liked all his neighbours and didn't want anything horrid to happen to any of them.

The fateful day finally arrived when Chris decided to go through Fiona's personal papers, letters, diaries; everything belonging to Fiona that Chris never touched since the accident.

Chris didn't know why she had suddenly opened her eyes, but she felt a voice begin to whisper in her ear whenever she took a drink. She didn't mention it to Stuart or Anne as she wasn't sure where this was going.

One afternoon, Chris walked nervously up the stairs and stood outside Fiona's bedroom door for ages before pushing the door open and just standing looking into the room that she hadn't been in since the accident.

After taking in all the memories that they had shared together in that room, she slowly ventured in and sat on the bed for what seemed like ages, immersed in Fiona's smell which seemed to be still hanging in the air. That couldn't be right but that was what Chris felt so she went with it. She lay down for a while trying to catch – what? something, some scent, some spirit, that was definitely still in the room.

When she felt at peace she got up and stared around the room, then started opening drawers and cupboards, just looking, until she felt it was the right time to touch the items that her beloved had touched.

Chris felt very nervous when first she opened Fiona's boxes, but that feeling melted as she began to feel closer to Fiona, and loved touching all her papers and personal items.

'I should have done this before, why didn't I? Fool that I am. I think you wanted me to, didn't you Fiona? But I wasn't listening. I am listening now though, listening to everything you have to tell me.'

Chris spent hours going through Fiona's things and by the end of that day, she was so exhausted that she forgot to have a drink. The next day, she went back to the bedroom and kept reading and sorting things out. It seemed to take forever as Chris read and re-read everything, unable to believe half of what she read.

The diaries that Fiona had written were about when Chris and she met, with all the inner thoughts and dreams that she had about the two of them. It was almost like having Fiona back, discussing little things and big things that they used to laugh about. Chris forgot that she was alone. Reading the diaries was almost like having a conversation with Fiona.

A year later

It was another lovely day in Glenfield Court. At number seven, there was a hive of activity. Relatives, friends and neighbours were coming and going. There had never been so many people in the house, and Chris had to go out into the garden to get some space.

It had been a quick year since Chris had ventured into Fiona's bedroom. So much had happened during that time that she had to check herself to make sure she wasn't dreaming.

'Darling,' bellowed Stuart as he came round the corner of the house. 'There you are. I just knew you had it in you to give us another best seller, you didn't let your public down. You are absolutely marvellous! Would you like me to pick you up for the launch tomorrow?'

'Stuart, you scared me, I didn't know you had arrived yet. Although I appreciate everything my family and friends have done, I do wish I could have the house back for a little while. Could you see what you could do, please?'

'My darling Chris, for you anything, just leave it to me,' and Stuart went inside after taking a puff of his cigarette which he had been trying for months to give up. He had started when Chris went into decline after Fiona died as he didn't know what to do to get her back into circulation. After months of trying to nudge, budge and finally get her to write the best novel to date, he couldn't stop smoking, so at the moment he just accepted it, as long as Chris was back he could put up with the horrid vice.

Chris stayed in the garden until Stuart came back out and told her that they had all gone, for the moment. 'Don't be surprised if they come back later but I told them that you had phone calls to make to radio stations and needed quiet. Are you all right, Chris?'

'Thanks, Stuart, I really appreciate what you are doing. I'm glad that there is just the two of us now, as I need to speak to you. I know I haven't been open with you these past few months, but I had to get something right in my head first and I think now is the time. Would you sit down, Stuart, please.'

They both sat on the chairs on the patio under the shade of the big umbrella that one of Chris's relatives had put up so that she could have a breather outdoors when she needed it. It had certainly come in handy.

Stuart didn't like the sound of what Chris was saying. He couldn't imagine what she was going to say to him.

He knew that he had been her rock since Fiona died, but they hadn't really confided in each other. Stuart felt that maybe he should tell Chris things about Fiona that she didn't know, he knew she was ready to hear them, she was strong and she wasn't going to subside again, but he just had to be absolutely sure.

They sat facing each other and didn't speak for a few minutes, Stuart lighting up another cigarette and Chris looking up at the window of Fiona's room. The birds were singing, the sun was still out and there was a warm breeze, it seemed all was right with the world to the outsiders, yes, it was.

'Okay, Stuart, let me start – and please, don't interrupt me until I have finished. You will get your chance, but I must say this in one go. Otherwise, I may not get out what I have to in order to, I suppose, cleanse myself.'

'First of all, I would never have got through this past few years if it hadn't been for you. You believed in me, knowing that I had another best seller. I certainly didn't think so, but you seemed to see right into my soul and I let you. Thanks, Stuart, thank you.'

Chris got up and wandered around the patio for a few moments. 'Last year when I thought I could never come back, be a whole person again, I heard a voice tell me to go up to Fiona's bedroom and funny as it may seem, I heeded as it felt right. I spent hours, days, weeks in her bedroom, just sitting, lying on her bed, going through her cupboards, boxes, photos, letters and diaries.

'Yes, Stuart, I went through everything I could find, because I felt I had Fiona back by touching and reading all her personal papers. I didn't feel I was nosey; that it was none of my business to be doing that. It was my right, Stuart. I had loved her so much, like I had never loved anyone in my whole life, it was MY RIGHT!!! and no one is going to argue with me.

'Stuart, I couldn't have spoken to you about it last year, but I have now accepted it and writing the novel was the best thing that I could have done. I now know that Fiona was going to leave me. And you knew it too, didn't you, Stuart?'

Stuart nodded his head without saying anything – he would get his turn, as Chris had stated.

'When I started reading all her diaries and letters and cards it took me a little while to realise that I wasn't the only one that Fiona loved. She kept all her letters from her ex-husband, ex-lovers – male and female. It was a shock when I found out but I couldn't stop reading them. She was a very extraordinary person, everyone she came in contact with loved her. That is what I felt the first night I met her. It terrified me, I felt like I had fire crackers going off inside me. I was excited but scared and I just had to leave the club.

'For the next two weeks, I could think of nothing but Fiona. When she finally came round to see me she knew how I was feeling too, she had that effect on people and she knew it. She never left after that night and I thought I had found the one – but I was one of many for her and she was on her way to the next one, wasn't she, Stuart? Why couldn't she stay longer than five years with anyone she loved? Why, Stuart? Why? Was there something wrong with me or was it just the way she was? I gave her every-thing! I gave her ME !!'

Chris sat down, exhausted to have got everything off her chest to Stuart. She knew there was still more to say, but she had got the bulk of it out and she felt better.

Stuart got up and wandered around for a few more moments before lighting up another cigarette. 'I'm sorry

Chris, I promise, I shall give up smoking but allow me a few more today and I shall throw the packet away after. Well, Chris, when I saw Fiona look at you at the club that night, I thought, oh, no! What do I do now? I had known Fiona since we were kids, a whole gang of us went around together and we did everything together. We went hiking, sailing, cycling, holidaying, everything, we were more like brother and sister. When she went away overseas the first time, I was devastated, but I gradually got over it. I once told her that I hated when she went away as I loved her, she told me, "Stuart, you don't love me. I am not for you, I shall never settle down, ever, I love being in love for as long as it lasts and by my counting I shall be in love with someone every five years. It could be male one time and maybe female another time, but that is how I feel. I don't know how or why I feel it but I know it to be true and I can't fight it. To me, love is only for five years."

'Chris, please, believe me when I say this, I could no more tell you how Fiona would behave towards you than I could fly like a bird. First of all you wouldn't believe me and you would be angry with me and our friendship would suffer but most of all, how was I to know that Fiona wouldn't change and settle down with you?

'I did talk to Fiona, to get some idea about how she felt about you, but she was her usual stubborn self and she told me in no uncertain terms that I wasn't to mention it to you as one never knows what might happen and that she could have changed. We did have an argument and didn't speak for a few weeks, but I could see that you were happy, she was happy, all our friends were happy, except me, so what was the point? So we made up.

'She was married once, when she worked in France. Although she was really in love and he with her, it only lasted five years, she just got up one morning, told him that she had to go and wasn't coming back – she went and she didn't go back. I went over to France to try to explain to Pierre but after that one time we never heard from him again. Fiona just couldn't help herself, but no one ever hated her. They couldn't, she was just Fiona,' and with that Stuart shrugged his shoulders. He couldn't explain Fiona to Chris as he couldn't explain her to himself.

Stuart walked around the garden, lighting up another cigarette, giving both him and Chris a few moments to digest what he had just said. He felt better after that and when he came back to Chris they both hugged each other and sat down again.

'Thanks, Stuart. I think I knew what you were going to say and really there isn't anything else to say as we would be just going round in circles. Fiona was Fiona and that's that. I have something else to tell you, Stuart. I am selling this place and going back home. I have tried ever since Fiona died, but she is in every room and now, I don't want her to be. She isn't coming back, and if I can't have the real Fiona, I don't want her spirit. I have to move forward and seek for what life has in store for me. I know that there is plenty but I won't get it in this house'.

Stuart was flabbergasted. He hadn't seen this coming and he thought he knew Chris better than anyone. She was still keeping a lot inside her and he doubted if she would let it out. 'Chris, I can't believe this, I know better than to argue or to try to change your mind, but are you absolutely sure? I can't believe it!'

'Yes, Stuart, there is going to be a For Sale sign put up in the garden tomorrow. The sooner I get away from here the better. I am going to tell my family tonight and start moving my furniture the day after the launch of my book.

It is final, Stuart. Depending if I write another novel you shall still be my agent, Stuart. I would never leave you in that respect, but the way I am feeling at the moment, I don't know if I shall ever write again. This house made me an author and when I leave, I think my stories will stay here.'

Stuart couldn't say anything. He sat, trying to take it all in. In time he would agree with Chris, that leaving was the best thing that she could do. If she wanted to continue living a full life she had to leave the ghost of Fiona here. He had a feeling that she wouldn't write again, this house gave her the inspiration and when she left it would stay here. Maybe it was the ghost of the lady who lived here before Chris that was the real author.

There was nothing left to say for the moment and they both got up out of their chairs and walked into the house through the patio door.

Dark clouds were forming in the sky and a breeze had got up, making the leaves start falling from the trees in the garden onto the chairs that they had just vacated. If Chris and Stuart had looked out of the patio window they may just have seen the faint shadow of what appeared to be an old lady sitting at the table leaning on her elbow toying with a pen in her mouth.

The End?